I0574928

Freshly Dead

Ghosts of Carrington
Book 1

Maddie James

Sand Dune Books

FRESHLY DEAD

Ghosts of Carrington, Book 1

Maddie James

Freshly Dead
Copyright © 2011, Maddie James

Editor, Wendy Williams
Cover Art Design by Jacobs Inc, LLC.

Digital Release, First Edition, December 2011
2nd Edition March 2016
3rd Edition May 2023

Published by Maddie James, Turquoise Morning, LLC, DBA Jacobs Ink, LLC.
P.O. Box 20, New Holland, Ohio

Maddie's VIP Insider News

Be the first to get the news about my books—new releases, free ebooks, sales and discounts, sneak peeks, and exclusive content! Just add your email address at this link: https://maddiejamesbooks.com/pages/newsletter

Freshly Dead

A southern-fried comedy with a touch of romance, a side of mystery, a smattering of paranormal, and three crazy sisters....

All Mitzi Winston wants is enough money to pay this month's mortgage payment. That is the only reason she even considers the phone sex job. Ever since her husband's disappearance, she has held things together nicely—until recently. And now, well, she just needs the money.

Biting the bullet, she goes for the interview, only to find that the phone sex job isn't real and she's too late—not for the interview, but to save her husband. For there he is, dead on the floor, a bullet to the back of the head. To make matters worse, his ghost is hovering around and chiding her for being late. Not to mention he is horny as hell and trying to cop a feel.

Which only begs the question, "Do dead men still want it?"

CLASSIFIED ADS:

Employment Wanted

SEX.

Now that I have your attention, I am looking for employment. Outstanding background in sales and marketing. College degree. Open to anything short of murder. Call Mitzi. 555-236-9435

Chapter One

"What do you mean I can't? I can do anything I damn well please." Mitzi Winston slammed her purse on the counter and twisted to look at her sister.

"It's illegal. You can't."

"Oh hell. Who would know? Besides, I need the money."

"Obviously."

"I don't need sarcasm, little Miss Rich Sister. I need dollars. The mortgage is due. Final notice. I'm not about to lose my house."

That was an understatement, to be sure. She stared out the kitchen window to look at the garden. The house was the only good thing she'd done in years. Finally, she had finagled a loan, scraped up the down payment, and became a homeowner. She wasn't about to stoop to renter ranks. Again.

"I'll give you the money."

"No."

"But—"

"I. Said. No." She didn't need handouts. Ever since Ken

disappeared, she'd made it just fine—until the bottom fell out of her freelance public relations business.

Suddenly, her clients started dropping like flies, leaving her in a lurch. And she couldn't get a contract job, even a small one, for anything.

Everything. Gone.

Just like Ken.

"It's just phone sex, Molly. It's not like I'm going to catch a disease. No one will know me. I'll tuck myself into my little bed and just talk guys into getting their jollies off. I'll be a hundred bucks richer every fifteen minutes. That's four hundred dollars an hour. If I get them off sooner, my income goes up. Piece of cake."

"You can't be serious."

"I'm dead serious."

"I'd have to be dead to do that."

Mitzi figured that Molly, after birthing three children, and putting up with that husband of hers, was pretty much dead tired when it came to sex anyway. "We'll, you're not me."

"The cops listen in on those things, you know."

"What two consenting adults do on the phone is of no concern to anyone."

"They try to catch johns and hookers."

"I'm not a hooker."

Molly raised a brow. "What would you call it then? A guy creaming in his jeans. You get money. Hooker. You."

"I wouldn't even touch them!"

"Mitzi! Listen to yourself!"

"And sometimes it's not guys. Women do it, too. Talk to other women."

Molly clapped her hands over her ears. "Lalalalala! I do not want to hear anymore." She grabbed her Gucci purse, the turquoise one that Mitzi had coveted for a month.

Damn her.

In two seconds flat, Molly whipped out a credit card. "Here. Or I won't be able to live with myself."

Mitzi swallowed her gumption. Probably thousands of dollars on that thing. Enough for the payment. Get her through until next month.

Damn.

"I can't." There. She said it.

Molly rolled her eyes. "I'm leaving."

She reached for Mitzi's hand, slapped the card down in it, and held her gaze long. And, believe you me, Southern girl steel magnolias could hold a stern gaze like, forever.

It was damned uncomfortable, but Mitzi held her own.

Then Molly left.

Her shoulders slumped. Damn that card felt good in her hand. But she would *not* use it.

* * *

The message on her answering machine said to show up at eight o'clock the next evening in the upstairs office at 3245 Halifax Street in the Juniper Hills area of Carrington, which was fortunate for Mitzi, since that was her hometown. No sign, he said, just walk on up and knock on the door at the top of the stairs. The one on the left.

Someone would be there.

Yeah.

It seemed a bit late for a job interview on a Friday night, but she figured the phone sex business was hopping around that time of day. She brushed away any niggling doubts.

The area was familiar, but she couldn't say she'd frequented it much in her lifetime. Suffice it to say Juniper Hills represented the seedier side of town, was mostly industrial, and sat on the wrong side of the tracks of this small Southern city in the heart of Louisiana.

Her daddy—even though she was well into her thirties—would go after her with a switch should he find out she was contemplating working over there. The Newberry men were just protective like that of their daughters.

It felt a bit creepy, but Mitzi swallowed her spookies, peered up into the dark stairwell, and stepped inside.

No light?

She propped the door open with her hip and searched for something to keep it cracked while she took the stairs.

There. Half a brick.

She glanced at her watch. Late. Shit.

She wedged the brick between the door and frame, making sure it would not pop out. Getting locked in on the inside of this door was not an appealing thought. Turning, she looked up dark the stairwell. A rectangle of light lit the way up.

Problem solved.

Would this company consider her problem solving an asset? Or would they just consider her "assets."

Time would tell.

She took the stairs, stepped on something crunchy at the top, rapped on the door and glanced behind her. Dark corners. A shiver tripped up her spine. Would she really want to work here?

The door creaked open. Slowly.

Wait.

Mitzi took in the silence.

Wait longer. Silence.

No one said, "Hello?" or "May I help you?" or "Kiss my ass," or anything. Swallowing the spookies again, she pushed the door inward.

"Hello?"

Venetian blinds, mostly askew, were pulled down on the window opposite the door. No, wait. Jerked down? Torn. A triangle of light from the streetlight poked through.

Wrong place. Had to be in the wrong place.

Retreat.

Out the door. Down. Two steps. Get out.

Turn around. Please. Come back.

What? Was that a voice?

Turning, she saw that triangle of light penetrate the hallway onto the stuff she'd crunched earlier. Light bulb. Smashed.

Oh dear. Not good.

Come back, please.

Crap.

She climbed the two steps, swallowed, and pushed forward into the room.

Holy shit!

There was a dead guy on the floor.

A. Dead. Guy. On. The. Floor.

And... And his ghost was sitting in the chair next to him.

Ghost?

"Hello, Mitzi. Par for the course. You're late, sweetheart. And now I'm dead."

Ken?

Mitzi stumbled, catching her backside on the open door. "Ouch! Dammit." She rubbed her left hip.

"You always were a clumsy little tart."

She widened her eyes and bore straight through the form that used to be her husband. Yes, straight through. He was rather, um, translucent.

"Oh, freaking shit! What the hell is going on here?"

Ken rose. Like, levitated.

She scrambled a few more steps in reverse. "Don't come any closer, Ken. Uh, you are Ken, right?"

5

He snorted. "Of course, baby. Come here and give me a little smooch. Been a while, huh?"

"Like hell." She bolted toward the window with the torn blinds. "You keep your dead lips off me." Panic raced up through her, from gut to throat. What the friggin' kind of trick was this?

"I don't have cooties, Mitzi. I'm just dead. Freshly so, it appears. And it's all your fault, my dear, so you owe me."

The gall of that man. Dead or alive, he always thought she owed him.

"Not my fault you went and got yourself killed, Ken." She glared at him for a second or two. "How come you're talking to me for real now, when a moment ago you were sort of like a voice in my head?"

Ken shrugged. "I'm not really up on the ways of the dead yet, hon, but I think it might have something to do with you looking at me and actually acknowledging me being dead. Something like that. I don't know for sure. I'll have to consult the dead experts around here."

Mitzi glanced about, the tiny hairs on the back of her neck rose. "There are more dead people than you in this room?"

"Perhaps. This place has a certain history."

She backed up. "This is truly a conversation I do not want to have."

"Oh," he interrupted. "And about that *you getting me killed* thing. Actually, it is your fault. You see, you were an hour late. If you had arrived on time, the plot to kill me would have been foiled. Why do you think I left that message on your machine? I needed you here at eight o'clock." He glanced at his watch. "Thought you might be respectfully early for your interview. However, I should have known that given your penchant for a grand entrance, not to mention your addled sense of time, you'd be slightly tardy."

Mitzi shook her head to clear a few grappling cobwebs. This was just too surreal. "I came not more than five minutes late. It was eight-o-five when I glanced at my watch."

"Beg to differ, love. It was nine-o-five."

"No way."

"Time change, sweetheart. You always forgot to set your clocks when the damn time changed. Your fault. You ruined the plan. And now I'm dead."

Mitzi contemplated that for a second. Shit. Had she been an hour behind all week? Never mind. It didn't matter. What mattered was that a dead Ken, her estranged and missing husband of two years, was lying in an expired heap on the floor (Crap! Was that blood halo around his head growing?), and his mocking ghost was giving her the third degree.

"Wait. I came here for a job interview. You're telling me that it was you who left that message on my answering machine? No way."

"Sure. What a stroke of luck seeing that ad. I knew it was you the moment I laid eyes on it, and I knew that was the perfect way to get you out of the current mess we're both in... well, the one prior to getting myself killed. Which again, is all your fault...."

"What mess? I'm not in a mess."

"Not yet. I had planned to protect you, keep you out of it, but no... You had to go and foil things."

No. Oh no. Not getting involved in any of Ken's current messes. Time to vamoose.

"If you don't mind, Ken" she began, rounding the desk and eyeing him carefully while skirting the room toward the door, "I'll be leaving now so you can tend to your own...um, deadness."

He blocked the door. "So, what are you going to do, sweetheart? Leave me here to fend for myself? I mean, I really don't mind so much being dead, considering the circumstances, but we've got to do something about this body. I'm not sure I can move it by myself."

Dumbfounded, Mitzi shook her head. "That's your dead body and I'm not touching it."

In half a second he'd billowed toward her and stroked her cheek with his pseudo-flesh pointer finger. "You never used to mind touching me, sweet pea."

Mitzi shivered and jumped back. "Ack! Stop that! I am not into touching the dead, in any way, shape, or form. Abuse of a corpse is not my thing."

He dropped his arm. "Oh, hell, Mitz. I'm not talking necrophilia here. I don't think that counts with ghosts. But hell, sweetheart, it's been a long time and you look so good, so how about snuggling up a bit and running your hands over my—"

"Jesus Christ!" Mitzi bolted for the door. "I'm out of here."

She heard Ken's voice ramble behind her as she tripped and fell down the stairs. "I have an appointment with Him later, sweet, so don't get Him riled, taking his name in vain and all that. I don't think He thinks too highly of me right now, anyway..."

Cripes. She needed to get out of here and clear her head. Certainly, she hadn't screwed it on straight this morning. Or something. What the *hell* was happening?

She needed tequila. Now.

Chapter Two

"**A**nd there he was, standing there smug and proper looking, all freshly dead and everything, with that pasty pale face, and trying to order me around. Men."

Mitzi took a quick glance around the darkened bar and snatched up the shot glass of liquor the bartender just handed her. She licked the back of her hand, shook on some salt, lapped it clean away, then slammed back the hefty shot of tequila. Instantly, she bit into a slice of lime, shivered and gasped.

Marla, her other sister, the one who liked sex and tequila (thank God she had one sister who was normal), stared at her.

"What?"

"Freshly dead?"

"Yeah, like in just murdered."

"I think you need to lay off the tequila, sister."

"I'm tellin' ya...."

Marla glanced at her watch. "That's your third shot in... thirty minutes."

"I'm fine, Marla."

"Well, just watch it."

She reached up and grasped her sister's shirt collar to pull her face closer. "Mar, I just saw the real live freakin' ghost of my estranged hubby today. Don't hassle me about the shooters." She let go, and Marla sank back into her bar stool. "And he tried to kiss me."

"Ewe!" Marla shook, her face twisted into an oh-that's-so-gross look. "Fuck, Mitzi. That is so wrong."

Marla had such a potty mouth—but it went along with her personality.

"Tell me about it." She waved toward the bartender. His back was turned. Dammit.

"Mitzi, wait. This was Ken, right? Your alienated husband who left you with a wad of past-due bills, a string of repossessors gracing your doorstep, and who stole our grandmother's diamond ring? Ken, whom you have not seen hide nor hair of in almost two years? The Ken the bounty hunters said they couldn't find to serve him the divorce papers? That Ken? Dead and talking to you from some sort of ghostly form?"

Mitzi bit her lip and glanced away. "Yeah, that Ken, Marla. The stupid klutz. Gone and got himself killed. And right when he was about to give me a job. Damned stiff owed me that, too."

She looked back into her sister's face. "Job? You didn't tell me anything about a job. Why would you want to work for Ken? I'm not getting this...."

"Cripes. Don't give me that look. There are too many things to get straightened out. The thing is Ken is dead. But I can't be worried about that right now."

"What?" Her sister looked stricken with horror.

"Well," Mitzi countered, "he's not that bad off if he's sitting there in the chair and talking to me now, is he? I mean, he argued for, I dunno, an hour it seemed, about me being late for the appointment. Pissed me off."

Marla shook her head. "I... I'm not getting this, Mitz. Something is dreadfully wrong here."

"Deadfully."

"No, I said dreadfully."

"Damn right, it is."

"You have a big problem on your hands. What did you do with the body?"

Mitzi arched a brow. "Nothing. It's still there."

"What? You didn't report it to the police?"

She shrugged. "Nooooo, why should I? Ken looked happy as a clam to me. He might be just a spirit, but I don't think he needs that body any longer."

Marla grasped Mitzi's arm. "My darling sister. The man is dead. He was your husband. Least of all, even if he was a slimy, weasel of a bastard, he deserves a proper burial."

Mitzi jerked her arm away and turned toward the bartender, finally signaling another shot. He nodded her way. "Knock it off, Marla. The man is too nasty to die. He's got something cooked up. I just know it. He's faking it. I know, maybe he was a hologram. No, couldn't be. There was a ton of seepy blood. But that spirit of his lives on. Stubborn son of a bitch."

"So, what are you going to do?"

"Do?"

"Yeah."

"I'm not going to do anything but try to figure out how I can get back what Ken owes me, and then I've got to find a job. A real one that doesn't include sex and telephones."

"Excuse me?" Marla's brow knit.

Mitzi waved her off. "Later. Just another chapter of the story. The thing is the bastard is back in town. He skipped out on me with some of my hard-earned cash and a credit card and yeah, Gran's ring. And I'm not over that car repo thing, either.

Not to mention I'm about to lose my house. The man owes me. I'm going back to set things square with that asshole."

She picked up her purse and headed for the door. Stumbled, actually. "Even if the son of a bitch is dead." What the hell?

Marla's hand firmly grasped her bicep. "Oh no, not tonight, Sis."

Mitzi watched her sister through blurred eyes as she shoved a few bills toward the bartender. Something was seriously wrong with her eyesight. The man looked awfully fuzzy. Dead-like. Ghoulish.

Was he dead, too? She grasped her tummy. Ewe.

Am I dead???

She dizzily whipped around to face Marla. "Am I dead!" she shouted.

It seemed everyone in the bar stopped talking and looked at her. Marla grasped her biceps. "No, dear sister, you are not dead. You're drunk. Now, lower your voice, please."

Not feeling so hot. Maybe it is time to go home. "Okay."

"C'mon," she heard Marla say from somewhere far and distant. "Time to go, wife-of-a-dead-guy."

* * *

The numbers on the clock radio beside her head read two-thirty-three—in the morning, Mitzi assumed, since the space all around the clock was dark.

Groaning, she rolled flat on her back and stared at the ceiling. Hell. She was drunk. Still. Or seriously hung-over.

Had she hallucinated this entire crazy episodic evening? Getting the call about the job? Finding Ken lying like a dead duck on the floor of that grimy office? His ghost virtually coming onto her?

Do dead guys still want it?

Ewe.

And then the tequila. Christ. That was it. Blame it on the tequila.

Someone groaned next to her.

Shit! What?

Ah. Yes.

Marla's place.

Her sister let out a soft snore as if to verify that fact.

They'd come back here, discussed The Ken Factor a while longer, while they chased down another few shots of tequila with a couple of cups of Cherry-Limeade from the drive-in down the street. That's what they decided to call the situation— The Ken Factor—rather than talking about him being dead in public.

If she squinted hard enough through the dark of the room, she could make out the ceiling fan hanging above Marla's bed. Crap, she just wanted to go back to sleep and forget this day.

You've left me in one helluva mess here, Mitz. You gotta help me out.

She widened her eyes. That sounded like Ken. In her head.

Couldn't be Ken.

Cripes.

Was he here? All spirit-like and everything?

No. Of course not, she argued with herself.

Silence.

No, I'm not there, not in my body anyway. I'm rather stuck though, Mitz, right where you left me. So c'mon, baby. Help me out here, huh? I can't seem to leave.

No. No, no, no.

Please?

Hell.

Mitzi rolled toward her sister. "Marla." She shook her shoulder. "Wake up."

"Hm?"

Her eyes were adjusting to the dark now. Marla's lids fluttered. "How drunk are you?"

"Deliciously drunk. You?" she murmured and rolled toward her, cuddling her pillow.

"No. Just stupid drunk, I think." She sat up and flicked on a table lamp, then reached for the phone while scratching her head.

Marla perched herself up on an elbow, squinting. "What day is this?"

Mitzi thought for a moment. "Um. It's Friday. No. Early Saturday morning."

"Good. I can sleep in. No school."

Marla spent her days teaching middle school English. Best damn middle school teacher in the school if you asked her. "Yeah. Good thing." Mitzi yawned.

"Who are you calling?"

"A cab."

"Why?"

"We have to go back and help Ken. Move the body." Mitzi wondered about the sanity of that statement.

"Crap."

"I know."

"Why now?"

She set the phone down in her lap. "Because he said please."

Marla rolled herself to an upright position and rubbed her eyes. "Nothing about this sounds like a good idea to me. But hell, let's do it. Ghostbusters ain't got nothing on us chicks."

Mitzi wasn't sure if Marla being into this was a good thing, or a bad one.

"But we can't call a cab."

Mitzi fiddled with the phone and pinched the bridge of her nose. "Why? We certainly can't drive in our condition."

"No, but we can't drag Ken's dead body out of a loft on Halifax Street and into a cab now, can we? We need another mode of transportation. Call Molly."

"Oh, crap, Marla! Molly? Why not just call Mom? Their lectures are rather interchangeable. Besides, I've already had my Molly fix for the day."

Marla glanced at the clock radio. "It's tomorrow. You had your Molly fix yesterday. You're due another."

"Shit."

"She can get Don's Hummer."

"As if that isn't going to be inconspicuous." Molly's hubby, Don, collected vehicles like they were Matchbox toys...and Mitzi was pretty darn certain Don would not relinquish any of his toys to his accident-prone wife. At least not knowingly.

"Got a better idea?" asked Marla.

"What about her caddy?"

"The lavender one? I'm also pretty sure a lavender caddy on Halifax with Marty Lyn makeup license plates and bumper stickers would be inconspicuous." Molly had made a shit ton of money selling Marty Lyn products.

"The trunk is big. All I was thinking," Marla tossed back, "But of course you are right."

The women stared at each other in silence. Then they finally said in unison, "The Grave Dodger."

* * *

Nearly an hour later, after several strong cups of coffee and cold showers to sober themselves up a bit, Mitzi watched Molly pull up in front of Marla's apartment in a custom designed, black four-wheel drive Ford F-450 Super Duty pickup truck, sporting equally black tinted windows and an extra helping of chrome, plus monster wheels and tires that elevated the truck oh, about two feet higher than normal. Their sister was short, barely five-foot-two, and Mitzi was almost certain that Molly was probably sitting on a phone book or something while trying to drive that thing. Could her feet even reach the pedals? Her head bobbed slightly above the dash as she peered over the steering wheel.

Oh crap, could she really drive that thing? Then as if to confirm the answer to her query, Molly rolled and bumped into the curb and jolted up over the sidewalk to a choppy halt, just like any other helpless Southern belle who could barely drive a stick would do.

Mitzi and Marla both jumped.

"That redneck husband of hers is gonna shit if we put a scratch on that thing," Marla said. "Is it even street legal?"

"No clue."

Marla grumbled something unintelligible back.

The ghoulish shadow of silver that graced the side of the truck was barely visible in the dark, although her stomach panged for an instant at the apparition. Given the choice of lavender caddy, humongous Hummer, or the four-wheel drive pulling truck, Mitzi figured they'd made the least conspicuous choice earlier. Now, she wasn't so sure. Besides, the ghost figure painted on the side suddenly gave her the heebie-jeebies.

"It will keep Ken company," Marla retorted as if reading her thoughts.

"What?"

"The Grim Reaper there." She nodded to the side of the truck.

"Cripes, Marla. Quit being so morbid."

Her sister turned to stare at her. "Morbid? Honey, we passed morbid a while ago." She glanced toward the truck, idling at a low rumble in the parking lot. "Okay, so she's here. Let's go get our man, er, ghost, er, dead body. Something."

"Cripes."

"I wonder what stage of rigor mortis he is into by now." Marla bit her lip.

Molly walked toward them, a deep scowl on her face.

"Stiff, I'm sure," Mitzi murmured.

Marla turned. "If I remember correctly, he was always stiff, right?"

Mitzi caught the sly wink at that statement. "Don't."

"Hey, Mitzi, I wonder how stiff a dead guy's thing gets when he's really dead?"

Mitzi punched her sister. "Gross. Stop it!"

Staccato footsteps broke though the night, bringing Mitzi back to the situation at hand. Heels. Molly had worn heels. Great.

"What the hell am I doing here in the middle of the night, interrupting my beauty sleep, having stolen my husband's truck? Hm?" Molly stood hands on hips before them, the diamonds on her fingers sparkling in the streetlight, her auburn hair perfection-coifed, her black eye-linered eyes narrowed and peering at them. "I mean, my God, I broke a nail getting out of the garage."

"You said you would be here in thirty minutes, Molly. You're late."

Mitzi admired the heck out of her older sister Marla, who didn't take any shit off Molly. Being the baby, Molly nearly always got what she wanted in life and made no bones about the world needing to turn on her axis.

"I couldn't find the right clothes."

Mitzi threw up her hands. "Hells bells, Molly! We're not going to a fashion show. We're picking up a dead guy."

"Ewe!" Molly's eyes widened, and she clapped a hand over her open mouth. "What?"

Marla put a calming hand on her forearm. "Relax. Not a big deal. It's Ken, and we're just going to help him out."

Molly's

Molly's eyes widened even more. Mitzi wasn't sure that was possible. "Ken?" She glanced at Mitzi. "Your Ken? Dead? The one who abandoned you and cleaned you out of everything you owned and...did you ever get Gran's ring back? That was supposed to have been part of my inheritance."

Mitzi hooked her arm into her younger sister's. "No, I didn't get Gran's ring back and, yes, that Ken. My old Ken. He's dead, actually, but needs our help, sort of." She nodded to Marla, and they started walking toward the truck. How did one explain the bizarre turn of events this evening in a brief conversation? One didn't. They would just have to fill her in on the way downtown. "Now, just give the keys to Mar and we'll get you the details. This shouldn't take long. You'll be back snug in your bed before sun-up."

Molly walked with them like an obedient puppy, her gaze raking back and forth between her two sisters. "I'm more worried about having Don's truck back in the garage before he leaves for work. But—Ken? Ken is dead? I really don't like dead, girls."

Marla patted Molly's arm again. "Me neither, but tonight, we gotta like dead—or at least pretend to—because we are going to be doing dead quite soon."

Mitzi pondered that. "I have no clue what kind of mood Dead Ken will be in when he sees the likes of you two, seeing that none of you got along very well...."

"Say what?" Molly's face went all puzzled.

Marla stopped and looked at Mitzi. "You're right. I never liked the son of a bitch, but if helping him out helps you get back what he owes you, then I'm all for it."

"But he's dead. What does he care? He won't know we're there picking up his dead body." The younger sister picked at her broken nail.

"Um," Mitzi began, "Oh, forgot one detail, Moll. You see,

Ken *is* dead, but his ghost is hanging around. So yeah, he'll know we're coming, and he'll see the two of you."

"Excuse me?" Molly's brows arched like McDonald's famous arches. "Ghost?"

"Spirit, what have you. He's hanging around. Can't leave until we move the body, etc...."

"Can he talk?"

"Yes."

Molly pondered that. "Good. Maybe he'll tell us where Gran's ring is."

Mitzi rolled her eyes. If she ever got Gran's ring back, Molly sure as hell wasn't getting it. Gran had given that to her personally before she kicked the bucket. But that was not an issue to get into tonight. "Yes, honey, we'll see about getting that ring back." At least this way Molly might be more, um...cooperative.

They arrived at the truck. Marla opened the door and shoved her two sisters inside, Mitzi first, Molly in the middle, should she decide to bolt, and Marla driving, of course.

Chapter Three

"So basically, that's it. I went to my interview last evening, you know, the one you didn't want me to go to, Molly? And when I arrived, there was Ken, all spirit-like and everything, sitting in a chair, same old Ken look on his face, staring at this bloodied body on the floor and acting horny as ever."

"Ewe"

"I know."

"I didn't know ghosts could be horny," Marla commented thoughtfully. "I just wonder...."

"Don't go there, Marla." Mitzi didn't even want to think about Dead Ken coming onto her again.

"I mean, remember the old movie *Ghost*? Patrick was sure horny...."

"That was a movie. This is real life."

"Or death."

"Unfortunately for Ken."

"So you just left him there?" Molly interjected.

Mitzi's shoulders slumped, and she looked across the cab at both sisters, the pair looking her way. "Okay! I should have done something, but I didn't. Scared the living bejesus out of me, I'll have you know, and I bet you would have done the same thing." She looked ahead at the dark empty street as they rumbled along. This damn engine was too loud. Why did they think this truck was a good idea? "Besides, we're going back now, that's what counts. Oh hell, it's raining."

"Probably a good thing," Marla commented. "Not many people will be out."

"My hair will get wet," Molly whined.

"Put a hood on it." Marla wasn't sympathetic. "By the way, did you put all that stuff I asked for in the back of the truck?"

"Mostly," Molly replied, "but that's when I broke my nail, and I had to go back to glue it."

Marla rolled her eyes. "Get the tarp?"

"Yes."

"Duct tape?"

"Uh-huh."

"Shovel?"

"A small one."

Marla arched a brow. "How small?"

"You know, one of those little garden hand jobbies."

"A trowel! You brought a freakin' hand trowel? How in the hell...." The truck engine revved a bit, and then Marla slammed on the brake, clutched and downshifted, jerking the truck to the side of the road, sending all three of them lurching forward toward the dash. Thank God for seat belts. "A trowel!" Her voice rose a couple octaves.

"Well, I got one for each of us!"

Marla lunged toward her sister. Mitzi knew she needed to jump in before Marla killed her. "Just drive, Marla. We'll figure the shovel thing out later. At least we got the tarp to wrap him up in." The rain started to pelt the roof of the cab now. All three sisters looked up.

"Hells bells," Molly whispered. "We're going to bury Dead Ken in the rain with hand trowels like we were planting pansies or something." She shivered a bit and stared ahead out the windshield. "Is this a dream?"

"Nightmare," Mitzi countered.

"Well, if someone had thought to bring a proper shovel."

Molly twisted to look at Marla, "You didn't tell me we were burying a body!"

"What the hell else did you think we'd be doing in the middle of the night with shovels and duct tape and a tarp?" Marla said with grit out of the side of her mouth.

"Drive, Marla. Now." Mitzi wanted this over before Molly came totally unglued. "We're just a couple of blocks away."

"Right."

"Dead Ken...trowel...pansies...Gran's ring...."

"Quit mumbling, Molly." Marla accelerated.

"That's right, just remember we're getting Gran's ring." If anything, sparkly jewelry could keep Molly's perspective.

"Gran's ring...pansies...."

Marla rolled on, and Mitzi leaned her head back against the truck seat and closed her eyes. In a couple of hours, this would all be over.

* * *

Fifteen minutes later the three of them stood in a misty rain, looking up the long dark stairwell toward the second story office on Halifax Street where Dead Ken waited. Marla held a bunched-up tarp in her arms, and Molly had the duct tape. Mitzi noticed the brick still wedged under the door where she'd jammed it earlier, forcing it open. She hoped that meant no one else had been by since she left.

"It's dark up there," Molly whispered.

Mitzi glanced to her right and up. "Out here, too." Then away from the building. "A streetlight is out over there."

"Spooky." Marla buttoned her coat up tighter at her chin.

"Is that window up there glowing?"

All three sisters looked up at Molly's question. Yes, an eerie green iridescence radiated from the second-floor office window.

"Bring your ghost buster kit, Mitz?"

"Shit."

"I wanna go home."

Mitzi linked her arm to Molly's elbow. "Nobody's going home until we get Dead Ken."

"Shit," someone echoed.

"Let's go. Now or never."

Molly turned to her. "Is never an option?"

"No."

"Then why did you say never."

Mitzi urged them forward. "I'll go first. Molly you get behind me. Marla, can you bring up the rear?"

"Sure thing, ghost sister."

"Shut up. I'm not dead."

"Let's hope it stays that way."

Mitzi put one step inside the landing of the stairwell and froze. What if....

What if the guys that killed Ken came back?

What if this was a trick?

She halted.

"What's the matter?" Molly bumped into her from behind, then Marla. Domino effect.

Mitzi shook her head. "Nothing."

Marla pushed both sisters forward. "It's raining harder, let me inside."

Mitzi moved up the first two steps. Her gaze lifted. Dark.

Green-tinged at the top. Molly's fists gripped the back of her jacket.

Come get me, baby. It's all right.

Ken. The lying, cheating, con-artist bastard. Could she really trust him? Didn't matter. At this point she wanted only one thing—to trust him long enough to get answers.

And money.

I better be getting something out of this Ken. Like a bucket load of cash. You owe me.

We'll talk. Just come get me.

Crap. How long has he been listening? *Why is it that you cannot just come to me?* Once again, Mitzi was bowing to Ken's needs, not her own.

I dunno, sweetheart. Has something to do with the body, I think. Seems like I'm sort of attached to it. Can't leave it...or it won't let me get too far away.

Double crap.

She rose three more steps, her entourage in tow. Molly tripped over her three-inch heels and lunged forward, pushing Mitzi down palm-first into the greasy, sticky carpet.

Ewe.

She didn't even want to know what that sticky was.

At the open doorway, a whoosh of icy wind raced up the narrow stairwell like the hounds of hell were upon them, moving with lightning speed through the corridor with a peculiar, whining screech, whipping their hair forward and pushing their bodies upward. The heavy door behind them sucked closed with a brain-shattering bang, thrusting them into complete darkness.

All three women screamed and scrambled to the top of the stairs, tripping one over the other, like the Devil incarnate was nipping at their fannies.

Chapter Four

"Shit!"

"What the freak?"

"I just peed my pants."

Wheezing and labored pants echoed throughout the small landing. Mitzi found herself crammed between the bodies of her two sisters, their arms tangled in some sort of frantic embrace.

"I can't stop shaking."

"Damn, it's dark."

"I know." Mitzi remembered that earlier there was a light in the ceiling. Even if she could find the string, the bulb was broken. She remembered that crunch on the landing.

"What the hell was that whoosh of something that just ran through here? One second I was cold and the other hot."

"Just the wind." Mitzi tried to peel one sister off her at a time. One of them was dripping on her. She sure hoped it was rain and not pee. "Someone, give up that death grip on my breast, please. Who's dripping?"

"Me. I got soaked bringing up the rear." Marla shook her

head, and more droplets flew. "There was no wind earlier, just rain."

She didn't want to think about that, but Marla was right. "Probably blew in quickly."

"Yeah, like a bat out of hell," Molly whispered.

"Hell. Don't talk about that."

"We're probably going to Hell for tampering with a dead body. What do they call that?"

"Abuse of a corpse. You don't go to Hell for that, just jail."

"Same difference. They don't have makeup either place."

"Jesus." That from Marla.

Molly kneaded the sleeve of Mitzi's jacket, her fingers sweaty and hot. She could feel it through the fabric. "You think that door will open back up down there?"

"Sure it will."

"I think I'll go find out."

Mitzi jerked her back. "No one's leaving until we all leave."

"It's dark up here, Mitz. How are we going to—"

At once, the landing filled with light. Mitzi looked up and saw the lone light bulb hanging down from the fixture in the ceiling. The one that was broken earlier.

"Well, I'll be damned...."

Then her gaze dropped toward the door opposite them, the one she'd entered earlier when she'd arrived for the job interview. The one behind which Dead Ken lay in wait then—and probably still did now.

It swung inward with a slight creak.

Molly clutched Mitzi's shoulder. "My heart is in my throat. Goddamn. I can feel it," she whispered. She grabbed Mitzi's chin and forced her to look at her, pointing to her throat. "Look at me, dammit! Do you see my heart beating right here up in my throat?"

Marla squared herself in front of Molly. "Let go of her, Mol.

And get a grip. Just remember. Gran's ring. Gran's ring. And revenge. We're getting revenge for our sister."

Molly nodded. "Gran's ring. Revenge. Got it."

Marla stared into her eyes. "You okay?"

She nodded.

Then Marla looked at Mitzi. "It's your show, sister. I say go for it. Lead the way."

Mitzi swallowed hard and nodded. "Follow me."

She stood frozen to the spot.

"We're waiting, Mitz."

She jerked her head. "Just getting perspective." Earlier in the evening, retrieving Ken's dead, and likely now stiff, body seemed a simple enough task. Now, she questioned the sanity of that decision. And why was Ken so silent suddenly? Three minutes earlier he was in her ear. Now, nothing.

Except, maybe, it was he who had turned on the light?

No matter. Just move forward, Mitzi. Get the body and get out of here.

"Follow me," she repeated.

"Oooooohhh..." a deep voice wailed from behind the door. Luring.

Molly screamed and grasped the hair on the back of Mitzi's head in two fists.

"Stop it! Just stop it!" She whirled toward her sisters, extricated her younger one's fingers from her hair, and then lunged toward the door. "It's just damn stupid Ken. And I've had about enough of this ghost shit, so..." She pushed ahead, her sisters still planted to the floor behind her, and with balled fists stormed toward the room looking for Dead Ken.

She shoved the office door fully back with a bang.

"All right, you bastard. I'm here. Now get your ghostly ass over here and help me rescue your frickin' body!"

Ghost Ken sat hovering over the wooden chair, almost in

exactly the position she left him. Dead Ken still lay on the floor, the halo of blood around his head larger now and stickier looking. Congealed?

"That took long enough."

Mitzi looked at her estranged hubby, the floating one, and sighed. "God, Ken, you are such a pain in the ass."

"And I have a feeling I will continue to be so."

"Hmpht. No doubt."

"So now that you are here, let's get down to business. Get us out of here."

"Us? As in, you and me, sweetheart, or as in you, me, and dead guy here makes three?"

Ken stroked his chin. Hm. Even mannerisms from life still manifest themselves in ghostliness, she guessed. That was always Ken's 'I'm thinking' gesture. "We all need to leave. Me, the body, and you. Not safe here. I can't seem to move my newly acquired self in this form away from the room. Not quite sure what it means in the spirit world, but I feel a strong compulsion to get this body out of here. I can't leave it behind. But there also is this other very strong spirit-like urging that tells me I have to go—and go soon."

Mitzi chuckled. "Ken, sweetheart, your soul always told you to run. What's new?"

"Danger."

She laughed aloud then. "Danger? Ken, you're already dead."

"True." He nodded. "But you're not. Getting my dead body out of here and moving my spirit has everything to do with your safety, love, not mine. Believe it or not, this time I am very concerned about you."

A sliver of icy-hot fear cut a frisson down her spine.

"Me?"

The sisters tumbled into the room. "Mitzi?"

30

The trio then followed with a spattering of words and phrases to no one in particular.

"Look. Blood. Ewe."

"God. I'm gonna puke."

"Christ. He's really dead. Isn't he?"

"Poor Ken."

Mitzi couldn't take her eyes off her ghost-husband. His gaze bore back with precisioned hardness. He whispered, "Yes, love, you're not safe. Your sisters either, not that I'm really interested in saving their asses, but for your sake, I'll include them, too. We all must get out of here. I'm sorry for getting you involved, but it's true. I'm in a bit of a pickle and so...."

"Shit." The oath was a bare whisper from her lips. How long would Ken and his shenanigans follow her? Even in life after death?

Apparently so.

Marla sidled up beside Mitzi, her gaze glued to the dead body. "Somewhere along the way I lost the tarp. I think it's in the stairwell."

"Get it. Take Molly with you. Be quick about it."

"But—"

"Now!" She looked her sister straight in the eyes. "Now, Marla, we have to make short work of this."

Marla lingered only a second then grasped her protesting sister's arm and dragged her away.

"They can't see me or hear me."

Mitzi whirled. "What?"

"Only you can see me like this. Or talk to me."

She huffed out a breath. "Lucky me, huh?"

"Could be."

All at once, she wanted to collapse into a small ball on the floor and curl into a fetal position.

Heavy footfall and the rustling of tarp moved back up the stairwell. Out of breath, Marla announced, "Got it."

Mitzi turned to her sisters. "Girls, look at me and be very clear. Tell me everything you see in this room."

"What?"

"Tell me. What do you see?"

Molly started rattling off, "A desk, stuff on it, Dead Ken, a table over there, a wooden chair."

"Stop. What about the chair? What's on it?"

Molly shook her head. "Nothing."

"Hovering over it?"

Marla cocked a brow. "Hovering over it? Nothing, Mitzi. Do you see...is Ken...like, here?" Her eyes grew round as Molly's hoop earrings, and she visibly swallowed hard.

Mitzi glanced back, and Ghostly Ken winked at her. "No," she said softly. "He's not. Never mind." Then at once she turned back to them. "What do you think? Lay the tarp out on the floor and then roll him over onto it?"

Marla looked at Dead Ken then back to Mitzi as she bent to spread the tarp on the floor. Molly took hold of one end to help her. "I was kind of hoping to see Ghostly Ken," she lamented. "I want to give him a piece of my—"

The door to the hallway slammed with a bang.

Marla jumped. "Goddamn!"

"Just shut up, Marla. Not the time to play give-Ken-a-piece-of-your-mind. Remember, he's a spirit, and I'm not sure how he'll react to anything these days."

Molly whimpered, "Is he, holy crap, here?"

Mitzi looked long and hard at her sister. "Could be. But let's get to work and get this body out of here, and we'll worry about Ghostly Ken and our next steps later."

"I'm not touching that bloody head." Molly scrunched up her face.

"Not asking you to."

Mitzi crouched and took a closer look at Ken on the floor. He was face down and the pool of blood appeared to be coming from both the front and back of his head. The entry wound looked to be just above his neck, where a small circle with oozing blood, now rather thick and gooey, ringed it. Of course, she didn't really know, not being a forensic person and all, but she had watched quite a bit of Crime TV.

She had the awful feeling that when they turned the body over, the exit wound would be a bit messier. Poor Ken. His face was probably half blown off. Had this been an execution style killing?

She shuddered at the thought and reached out to stroke a lock of his long black hair. He'd always worn it rather shaggy and near shoulder length. Funny, it was still silky on her fingertips. How many times had she run her fingers through his hair?

God, she hoped he didn't suffer long.

Don't think about it sweetheart. It was quick. I promise.

She jerked back her hand. "I'm not thinking anything."

Ken scoffed. *Yeah, right.*

"Stop it, Ken."

"What?" Marla asked.

Mitzi shook her head. "Nothing. Let's do this thing, okay?"

Molly stood, hands on hips. "We're ready. The tarp is all spread out."

"Got the duct tape?"

"Yep."

"Marla, come over here and help me." Mitzi stayed crouched next to the body. "On the count of three, we roll him over and onto the tarp. Then Molly, you throw the other side over him. As quickly as we can, let's wrap the duct tape around him and get him down the stairs. Got it?"

"Yeah."

She looked first at Marla then Molly. "Good. Oh, and just fair warning when we roll him over, I wouldn't look at his face. I have a feeling it isn't pretty."

Molly wrinkled her nose.

Mitzi slid her hands under Dead Ken's body and grasped his shirt. Marla followed suit. "On three. One. Two. *Three.*"

With a grunt, the two women rolled the body onto the tarp.

"Ewe," all three echoed when Dead Ken flipped over onto his back and their gazes involuntarily moved to his face.

"Oh. That had to hurt."

Then Mitzi looked lower to his center region where Ken's trousers were obviously...um, tented.

Marla must have noticed it too. "Whoa, Ken. Is that a banana in your pocket or are you just happy to see us?"

Ken snickered in Mitzi's ear. *Sorry, sweetheart, but I was anticipating seeing you when I was inconveniently offed.*

"Shut up," she grumbled.

"Excuse me?" Marla responded.

"He's stiff," Molly commented.

"No joke," Mitzi countered. "Give me that duct tape, and let's get the hell out of here."

"Are you sure we have enough tarp to cover that, um, level of stiffness?"

Mitzi gave Marla a sarcastic look, shot her the bird, then flipped the tarp over Dead Ken. Unfortunately, the thing was still tented. "Hand me that damned duct tape."

Chapter Five

"God, he's heavy."

"His pointy thing is touching me. Can we turn him over?"

"His pointy thing?"

"You know. The banana in his pocket."

"Turn him toward Mitzi. She's used to his pointy thing."

"Would you all just shut up? Marla, lower that tailgate. Can you do it with one hand? We probably shouldn't set him down."

"Damned straight. I don't think I could heft him up again."

"Tail gate down. Heave ho."

"Be gentle."

"Christ, he's dead!"

"Watch out for his pointy thing."

"Ewe."

With a hefty hoist, Dead Ken tumbled onto the truck bed with a thud, and Marla slammed shut the tailgate. "Let's get the hell out of Dodge."

"I thought this was a Ford." Molly paused.

Mitzi rolled her eyes. "Just get in the truck."

The sisters raced for the truck cab and climbed inside.

Marla started the engine and jerked away from the curb. Mitzi laid her head back against the seat and closed her eyes. Thank God, this part was over. Then straightaway, they flashed open again.

"Ken."

"What?"

"He's still back there." Marla shot a look over her shoulder.

"No. Um. Not...that one..." Mitzi spun to look out the back window. No Ghostly Ken was hovering over the body. "Crap."

"What's wrong?" Molly stifled a yawn with the back of her hand.

"I think we have to go back."

"Forget it, sister." Marla was definitely still moving forward.

Mitzi looked at her then turned around in her seat. Instantly, she encountered deep brown eyes set in a translucent form. Ghostly Ken was sitting in her lap!

Sh. Be quiet love. I wouldn't want to frighten your lovely sisters.

Mitzi felt relieved that they didn't have to go back and get him, then on the other hand, panicked just a tad at the thought of Ken's ghost sitting on her lap. And suddenly, he didn't look quite as translucent as he did earlier in the evening.

What in the hell am I going to do with you? She looked him straight into his baby browns as she asked the question.

We'll figure it out, sweetheart. And the process could be fun.

Shit.

"So where are we taking him? Did you think that far ahead, Mitz?"

No, she hadn't. "Give me a sec," she replied, then, "yeah, take him to Gran's house."

"I thought we were going to bury him?"

Somehow Mitzi didn't think that was good idea now. "No,

Gran had a big freezer, remember? We cleaned it out last fall. It's nearly empty. I think he'll fit."

"You're going to freeze him?"

It seemed like the right thing to do, although she didn't know why. "Yes. We're going to freeze him." And Ghost Ken wasn't objecting, so she felt they were good.

Funny how her lap felt all nice and warm and cozy, now. Was Ken touching her...?

No.

"So, I broke a nail for nothing looking for those little shovels?"

Mitzi knit her brow and looked at her sister. "Apparently so."

"Well, great."

"Look at it this way," Marla interjected, "no digging, no risk of future nail breakage."

"Oh, you're right. Of course."

"Besides, I have a feeling Ken might need his body intact in the future." Both sisters looked at Mitzi. "I know it sounds weird, but it's just a hunch."

Ken nuzzled closer to her as if in agreement. Could she really feel him nuzzling her?

U-uck.

"All right. Gran's freezer it is."

Molly gave a thoughtful glance to the truck bed. "Do you think we'll actually be able to close the lid on that pointy thing?"

Marla laughed, and the others followed suit. It was the first laugh they'd shared in a while.

* * *

At thirteen minutes until six a.m., Mitzi stood alone in her Gran's basement and peered down at a tarp-covered Dead Ken laying face up in the chest-style freezer. He was tucked in tight as a tamale wrapped in a cornhusk between bags of frozen blackberries Marla had picked last summer and a half-dozen packages of deer parts Molly's husband had stashed in there over the winter. The freezer had been nearly empty until deer season. She had forgotten about that. Gran's house and all it encompassed came in handy for all the Newberry granddaughters, occasionally. Of course, no one thought it would ever come in handy for hiding a dead body.

Mitzi looked over the tarped form as she prepared to close the lid. A pang of sadness shot through her chest, and her tummy tightened in a knot. Christ, you'd think she was closing the casket on him. Hm. In a way, she was. Thankfully, there was ample clearance for his pointy thing, she noted as she gently shut the freezer door.

Poor Ken.

She paused thinking about the events of the past day—half-day, really. What in the world had Ken gone and done that had gotten him killed? And how in the world had he involved her?

Her emotions ran the gamut of feeling sympathy for her murdered husband and rage at the fact that she'd finally found him, and that he was dead and couldn't help her out of the mess he'd left her in.

Or could he?

Hm.

"Wait until I get you alone, you sucker. I have a bone to pick with you."

"You can pick my bone anytime, sweetheart. Pick it, touch it, lick it...."

Mitzi swiveled away from the freezer and turned to see Ken's ghost standing behind her. The sight of him nearly took her aback. Either she was getting used to him being a specter, or he was becoming less ghost-like with every minute. At least in her eyes. Suddenly, all the reasons she was ever physically attracted to him came rushing back. He was the most handsome man she'd ever met way back when, and if the truth be known—even in death—he was still.

His longish black hair shimmered, reflecting light from the lone incandescent bulb suspended above their heads from the low basement ceiling. Suddenly she ached to run her fingers though his tresses again. Her gaze roamed over his face as he studied her as well. Chiseled features, brown-black, deep-set eyes, heavy brow, regal nose.

Damn, but he still did it for her.

"Stare much?" he taunted.

Mitzi blinked and looked away. No, she would not let him get to her. He was, after all, a ghost. Dead. She glanced back. "What is this all about, Ken?" There. Change the subject. That was safe. Her libido was playing tricks on her.

He moved forward. "Yes, I do suppose you need some answers."

"That would be nice." She crossed her arms and lifted her chin. A meager attempt to put up some sort of barrier, she supposed.

"Baby, I never intended that it get this far." He took another step closer.

"So how far is it?" She pushed herself backward and turned away. Too close.

But suddenly he was next to her ear, whispering. "Sweetheart, let me explain. It was a deal gone bad. I got into some heavy-duty underbelly work and ended up as a police informant."

Damn, could she really feel his breath on her ear?

For a moment, she closed her eyes and let a tingling sensation wash over her. She got a faint whiff of his aftershave. A sense of familiarity, of longing, took hold of her.

No.

Turning back, she examined his face. Yes, he was too close, but she needed to look into his eyes to know if he was telling her the truth. "What are you saying, Ken. That you are involved with the police?"

"Was. Two years ago, and yeah, up until yesterday."

"What?"

"I know. Weird, huh?"

Mitzi scowled and shook her head. "This makes no sense, Ken. You were a business owner. The restaurant was doing fine. We were doing okay financially. Your income allowed me to invest in my own business. Then one day you went to the races and, poof! It was all gone. You were gone. And my life turned to total shit. That's not weird. That's just plain crap!"

Ken stepped back and looked her over. "Ah, well, yes. From your perspective it probably was pretty shitty."

"Diarrhea shitty all over the place. My life for two years has been hell. It was all your fault. And now you owe me, you bastard."

"Mitzi, sweet, just let me explain, okay?"

The basement door at the top of the stairs opened with a pop and in an instant, Ken disintegrated before her. Molly called out, "Mitz, it's after six. I gotta get the Grave Dodger home before Don has a hissy fit when he finds I've taken it. He's been on a terror lately, and I don't wanna do anything to cross him."

Grave Dodger. She glanced at the freezer to her left and the empty space of air that Ken had occupied just seconds earlier.

"Sure, Molly." Last thing they all needed was Don Campbell, Molly's redneck husband, throwing a hissy fit, whatever that was. Weren't hissy fits usually reserved for older, hysterical Southern women?

Ah, well.

Damn, had she done the right thing by freezing him rather than burying him? She supposed time would tell. They just had to keep anyone other than the three of them out of Gran's basement.

Like, their mother, for one. Lord help them all should she stumble upon....

"Mitzi?"

"Coming." She took two steps up the stairwell then turned back. "Stay here," she whispered, hoping Ken would get her drift. She didn't need an apparition following her about all day long. Besides, she was fast approaching exhaustion and needed sleep. Soon.

Blissful, peaceful, uninterrupted sleep.

Yes.

* * *

Slowly, Mitzi came to awareness, her first thought of how wonderful it was to be sandwiched between the sheets of her own bed. She smiled and snuggled deeper into the nest of pillows she'd made for herself. Barely conscious, she breathed in the dryer-fresh, floral bouquet of the pillowcases, thankful she'd changed her sheets the day before.

Nothing better than waking up with spring-scented sheets. Yawning, she moved her arms up and out of the covers and stretched them far over her head as she turned over onto her back. Behind her closed lids she knew it was exceptionally light in her room and sensed the sun shining in from the west window. She managed to turn her head slightly and squint her eyes at the clock radio sitting on the bedside table. Nearly eleven a.m. She'd slept a few hours, thankfully. Turning away, she curled onto her side and into a satisfying warmth that wholly enveloped her.

She felt deliciously happy and content at that moment, like being wrapped in a balm of security and love. So much so that she fell back into a peaceful slumber—until a soft snore woke her.

Her eyes flashed open.

For a moment, she lay very still and sensed her surroundings, her face buried in her pillow. Then she felt the slight pressure on her back and the fingertip caress on the nape of her neck. A protective arm drew her close.

No.

She lifted her face slightly.

Ken's spicy aftershave wafted over her nostrils.

"Shit!"

Bolting upright, she took sheet and covers with her, and much to her dismay, revealed a naked Ghostly Ken lying beside her. Complete with hard-on.

"Yikes!"

"Oh, sweetheart." Ken startled awake, and all she could think of was, do ghosts really sleep?

"What the hell are you doing in my bed?"

He rose on one elbow, that come-hither, sleepy-lidded look in his eyes that she knew and loved so well—at one time in her life. No more.

"Get out!"

He reached for her. "Now, Mitz, just listen."

"Out."

"Sweetheart."

"Don't sweetheart me. I want your dead self out of my bed. Now I have to change the sheets again." She glanced at his erection, tried not to grimace. "And can you soften that thing up a bit? I mean, really."

Ken sighed. "Mitzi, I'm not leaving any sort of dead residue behind." Then he peered proudly down at his phantom phallus.

"I'm sort of relieved, actually, that being dead, I can still get it up." Reaching for his thing, he caressed it a bit between thumb and forefinger.

Mitzi shimmied and looked away. "Don't do that. I don't care if you aren't leaving dead residue behind," *and I hope no other kind of residue*, "I can't sleep in a bed with a dead man. Leave, please."

Resigned, Ken replied, "Sure. Just let me do one thing before I go, okay?"

Mitzi eyed him suspiciously. "What?"

His gaze caught hers and held for a macro-second, and then he scooted closer and lifted his right hand next to her cheek. "Just let me touch you. Just once more."

Cripes. No.

"For old time's sake?"

"Ken...uh, I dunno...."

"I won't hurt you," he whispered.

There are all kinds of ways to get hurt, Ken.

Electricity jumped between his fingertips and her cheek. Involuntarily she closed her eyes. "Just once," she squeaked out. Somehow she knew even with her eyes closed that Ken was smiling.

And still dead, of course, but she tried not to concentrate on that at this particular moment in time.

His fingertip stroke to her cheek was not unlike any other he had softly caressed over her face. She used to love when he would take both of his big hands, hold her face in them, then softly kiss her. Today, however, there was a different sort of current passing through from his spirit to hers. One that....

At once, the tingling current left her cheek and moved to her lips. She imagined Ken playing a thumb over her lower lip, actually, felt him rubbing and caressing at the same time, followed by.... Was that really his thumb on her lower lip?

Ah. Maybe not.

Lips.

His.

Warm.

Wet.

Sliding over hers. Sensations she'd long ago tamped well-deep inside her, boiling up and readying themselves to burst over in anticipation of more to come.

She opened her eyes.

Ken's closed eyes were right there. So close. As he kissed her. And she let him.

A crack and a shattering of exploding glass cut the kiss off entirely too quickly.

"Get down!" Ken ordered and rolled her off the bed onto the floor opposite the window. "Stay down."

Confused and disoriented, Mitzi did as he said, pulling a quilt off the bed to wrap herself up in as if that would offer her any protection. Ken was up, however, and somehow dressed now, and looking out the window.

"Gunshots?"

"Yeah."

"What the hell?"

"I don't know. Stay out of sight."

"Get away from there!" she hissed. "You'll get hurt."

Ken glanced at her and chuckled. "Seriously, sweetheart?"

"Oh."

"You just stay down. Let me do a quick survey around the house. See what I can see."

Then he was gone.

No more shots. No more window breakage.

No more Ken.

Typical.

Mitzi rolled up onto her knees and sneaked a peek over her

bed and out the window. Nothing. Quickly, she grasped her cell phone off the nightstand and dialed 9-1-1, ducking back down and pulling dirty clothes out of the pile on the floor to clothe herself. Suddenly, she found herself wondering just how much weirder her life could get. Like, waking up next to a ghost, letting him kiss her, then getting shot out of bed.

Yeah, all that was just freaking weird.

Chapter Six

A brisk knock echoed through the empty house. Mitzi swallowed hard and weighed the sanity of her reporting the shooting to the police, particularly since Ken had disappeared, and she had no idea when he would show up.

But no matter, the deed was done.

"I swear, you bastard, if you show up and cause trouble during all of this, I'll..." What? What could she do to him that was so bad? He'd already had his face shot off.

She exhaled long and pulled open the door. "Officer?"

He tipped his cap. "Ms. Winston? I'm here about your reported shooting."

"Yes. Come in."

He was all business, perched on the edge of her couch, spiral notebook in hand, pencil poised, gun strapped to his side, legs spread apart in a come-on-I-can-handle-you stance. Sitting ramrod straight, he didn't crack a smile. No-nonsense and cocksure was written all over him.

She didn't trust cops.

They went through the obligatory cop-victim banter.

Where were you when it happened? What were you doing? What did you see, hear, smell, feel, etcetera. Thing was, it was extremely difficult to respond when the answers that rolled around in her head were things like: in bed, kissing my dead husband's ghost, smelling his aftershave, staring at this dead hard-on, feeling his fingers caress my face, and wishing he wasn't so dead at the moment.

"I was sleeping," she replied. "The shot woke me up." It was sort of not a lie, right?

"Mind if I look at the crime scene?"

"Not at all." She led him through her living room and around the corner toward the master bedroom. *Please, Ken, if you are there, get out.* Not that the officer could see him, but she didn't want to be distracted. "Right through here."

Mitzi led the way into the bedroom and pointed at the window. A quick glance throughout the room told her Ken was nowhere to be found.

She slipped out a lengthy exhale between her teeth.

The officer looked at her. "You okay, Ms. Winston?"

She nodded, but his gaze lingered. It made her a mite uncomfortable, but she couldn't pinpoint why. He turned, and she watched as he perused the window and the area around it, including the bed. His gaze remained there, too, and some kind of warning sign rose inside of her, raising those tiny hairs on the back of her neck.

No. No way. He couldn't know that Ken was there. Right?

Were there two dents in the pillows?

Of course not. Ghosts don't make dents in pillows.

Do they?

"You were alone, Ms. Winston?"

Her gaze turned sharply to the officer. "Yes." Suddenly, her mouth went dry. He looked her over for another moment, and then he broke away and peered out the window again.

"Have you moved anything?"

She glanced at the comforter in a wad beside the bed. "Just the quilt. I kind of rolled over with it onto the floor."

He nodded. "Okay. Don't clean this up. I'll have someone come in here and sweep for evidence. Outside, too. I'm calling now."

He crossed the room and stopped abruptly near the door on the wall opposite the window. His eyes narrowed as he peered closer at a small hole in the wall.

"There's your bullet."

"What?" She leaned closer.

He looked at her. "Don't touch it."

"Of course not." She lifted her chin. "I watch Crime TV."

He chortled and moved through the hallway, pulling his two-way off his belt.

His stoic demeanor was rather off-putting, but she figured that was just the way cops were. Being that this was the first experience she'd ever had with a police officer up close and personal, except for those couple of speeding tickets, and the time she stole Rudolph off the neighbor's roof when she was thirteen (hey, it was a dare), and oh, the one who came by to talk to her when she'd reported Ken as a missing person two years ago, she really couldn't be sure. He walked off, back toward her living room. She stood in her bedroom doorway and watched as he paced while he talked in a muffled voice to someone on his radio.

Before she moved, Mitzi took a sideways glance at the bullet lodged in her wall and shivered. Then, her gaze lowered to her dresser just beneath the bullet hole. A stack of bills lay neatly placed underneath her favorite cologne. She pulled them out and counted.

Five hundred dollars.

What?

Where had the money come from?

Her gaze slid to the side of the bed Ken had just evacuated. "Did you leave this?" she whispered. Her heart softened at the thought. She curled her fingers over the bills and slipped them into her underwear drawer.

Somewhat bewildered, she left the bedroom and busied herself by making a pot of coffee in the kitchen.

Did Ken really care?

"I wouldn't stand near the window, Ms. Winston."

"Excuse me?" She had been staring out the window, hadn't she? Lost in thought, thinking about her garden and the spring flowers and how she wished she could just go out there and dig in the dirt and plant something. Not pansies. Not Dead Ken. Just pretty little things that reminded her of nothing like ghosts and bodies and gunshots and the like.

Looking down, she swirled the coffee in her cup. Had she offered him any?

"Coffee?"

"No, thank you. Back away from the window, Ma'am."

"Oh." She got it now. "Are other officers coming?" She was a little distracted.

"Yes, Ma'am, they are on their way." He took her elbow. "Now, if you don't mind, I have a few more questions."

She really wished he would just go and couldn't imagine any more questions about this morning that needed asking. "I believe you were pretty thorough earlier, Officer..." Suddenly she realized she had forgotten his name. Had he ever given it to her?

"Dryden."

"Yes. Officer Dryden."

"This way, Ma'am." His fingertips were still on her elbow. He led her toward the living room. "I have some questions about your husband."

Mitzi stopped dead in her tracks and jerked her elbow out of his grasp. A cold chill traveled her entire body and landed with a clankety-thud in the pit of her stomach.

She looked him square in the eye. "My husband?" Shit. Think, Mitzi. What in the hell did you give away?

"Yes. Your name and address in the database brought up a red flag."

"Red flag?"

"Um. Yes. His death."

Crap! Thinking...thinking....

"Murder, was it?"

"Ah, actually officer, he was never—"

"The death has gone unrecorded."

"That's because he was missing and never—"

An agitated knocking and shaking of her front doorknob interrupted them. "Mitzi!" The voice on the other side was frantic.

Mitzi looked at the officer. "My little sister." Thank God for small miracles. She rushed to the door and yanked it open. Molly stumbled through the doorway mid-knock, almost falling off her lavender Jimmy Choo stilettos. "I came as soon as I heard it on the police scanner," Molly yelled. "I know how you hate cops, and now I see a cop car—" She halted at the sight of Officer Dryden stepping up beside Mitzi. Eyes wide, her mouth snapped closed.

"Come in. I'll explain."

"What the hell is going on?" she bellowed and shook her hands in the air. "Are you okay? Is he here to arrest you because, like, you know, we were all in on it?" Molly glanced from her to the officer.

"Molly, calm down."

"I mean," she went on, "we're all accessories and—" She said it like they were scarves or something, and not people who had assisted with the crime.

"That's accessory." She emphasized the pronunciation and glared at her sister. "And we're none of the sort." Molly was a walking accessory (of the fashion kind).

"But we took the—"

"Stop!" Mitzi glanced at Officer Dryden. "I mean, Molly, sit down. Let me get a darned word in edgewise," she said sweetly, tossing the officer a saccharin smile.

Mitzi linked her arm with her sister's and dragged her toward the kitchen. "Let me get you some coffee, Molly." She looked over her shoulder. "Excuse us just a minute, Officer, while I calm my sister down. I'm sure she heard about," she glared into Molly's startled eyeballs and said loudly, "the *shooting* that happened here earlier this morning, and is talking hysterically. Some coffee will help."

By now they were in the kitchen and slightly out of sight of the officer. Molly pulled away. "Shooting?" she whispered.

"Yes."

"Coffee hell, give me a beer."

"It's barely past noon."

"I don't care."

"Got it."

Mitzi opened the fridge door and pulled out a cold Bud Light. She grasped the lapels of Molly's Marty Lyn lavender suit jacket, pulled her forward, and angled them in between the refrigerator and door, like it was a cone of silence or something. "Don't do or say anything stupid," she whispered, "do you hear me? Just follow my lead and keep your trap shut."

Molly took the beer and twisted off the lid, nodding. "I am so out of the loop." She took a drink. "Oh, good, with lime."

"Everything all right in here?" Officer Dryden stepped into the kitchen.

Mitzi stood with the refrigerator door open, her hand still on the six-pack. "Peachy. Beer, Officer?"

"No, Ma'am." He eyed the sisters.

Mitzi cleared her throat, and the two women stepped out of the Fridge of Silence and into the kitchen.

Officer Dryden's two-way crackled to life. He put his hand to his waist and turned up the volume, listening. After a moment, while Mitzi and Molly glanced about and pretended not to be listening, he said, "If you ladies will excuse me, my investigators have arrived." He looked directly to Mitzi then. "We'll need to look around for a while. Is there a time we can continue our conversation?"

She swallowed, her throat suddenly parched again. "Sure," she got out. "Do you need me to stick around, or can you catch up with me later? My sister and I have an engagement in a few minutes."

"Oh, my morning is—"

"Booked solid. I know, Molly. So, let's get those errands out of the way now."

"Err—?"

Mitzi pushed her sister toward the living room again. "Yes. Daddy's birthday, remember? The presents."

"Huh?"

Mitzi stared hard at her sister.

Finally, Molly winked back. "Oh. Yes. Daddy's birthday."

They hurried toward the door.

"Ma'am?"

Both sisters whirled.

The officer pointed to Molly. "Better leave the beer here, open container law and all."

"Oh! Silly me!" She sat the beer down on an entry table and practically fluttered her lavender self toward the door. "Bye!"

Mitzi looked Officer Dryden square in the eye and suddenly

realized she didn't like him. She didn't know why, it was just a gut thing. She didn't like him one bit. Molly tugged her elbow. "I have to go," she told him, and made a "call me" phone gesture with her thumb and pinky finger. "Call me about those questions, and oh, please lock up!"

At last, they left out of the house and hurried into the caddy to make their pseudo-getaway. Mitzi laid her head back against the seat, closed her eyes, and sighed as Molly drove.

"Wow, that was intense," Molly said.

"Let's talk about it later." Mitzi rubbed her forehead. Damn, she needed caffeine. Headache. "Can you stop at the Coffee Caper around the corner?"

"Sure."

"Thanks."

They rode in silence for a moment. "Mitzi, I—"

"Later, Molly."

More silence.

"One thing. Thank goodness you mentioned Daddy's birthday. In all the hoopla, I'd almost forgotten."

Mitzi opened one eye to look at her. "I said that to get you out of there before you revealed anything incriminating."

"But it is tomorrow, right?"

"It is?"

Molly looked at her. "Yeah? His birthday is tomorrow, but the party is...."

Both sister's shrieked and jerked their heads toward the other. "Tonight!"

"Argh..." Molly called out, looking back to the road, narrowly missing an old guy with a walker crossing Delaney Street against the light. "Mom changed it!"

"Hell." Mitzi slunk back and closed her eyes again. Her head now hurt like a mother-fudger. She did remember a mention of that earlier in the week. "Where?"

"At Gran's. I bet Mom is over their cleaning right now."

Mitzi sprang up off her seat about the same time Molly tramped on the brakes and skidded to a sideways halt right in front of the Coffee Caper.

"Shit," they said in unison. "Dead Ken."

Chapter Seven

"Code Blue! Code-frickin'-blue! Gran's house. Stat!" Mitzi screamed into her cell phone. "Move your ass, Marla. We're in the caddy. ETA ten minutes!" She watched a lot of Crime TV, but her first love was The ER Zone.

"Oh, crapola. Please do not let Mom get on a cleaning spree." Molly cruised down Main, skidded through a yellow light, and cornered Yarrow like it was nobody's business.

"Marla's on her way," Mitzi said, still holding the phone to her ear. "I have no clue, Mar! I didn't remember it was Daddy's freaking party tonight, did you? Who the hell's idea was it to hold his party at Gran's house anyway?"

Molly cleared her throat. "Actually, Mitz, it was yours. You said we'd have more room."

She fell back against the seat. "Hells bells. Drive this thing or pull over and let me do it."

In response, Molly tramped on the accelerator and breezed through a stop sign.

"I didn't mean get us killed!" She looked back at the intersection they'd just whizzed through. "Cripes."

Molly glanced into her rearview mirror. "Dammit."

Blue rotating lights bounced off her sister's face as she slowed and eased the caddy to the side of the road.

"I want to say a really, really bad word right now."

"If it starts with F, I know the one."

"Damn stop sign!"

"Calm down, Molly. Be sweet. Here he comes. Cry if you have to. Show him some cleavage. Take the ticket then get us the hell down the road."

Molly rolled her eyes and her window down at the same time.

"Why, hello Officer...."

Mitzi could swear her sister's eyelids fluttered at that moment.

"Driver's license, registration, and proof of insurance, please."

The officer leaned over to peer into the caddy. He looked briefly at Molly but then skidded his gaze straight across to Mitzi. "Ms. Winston, we meet again."

Shit. Dryden.

"Officer Dryden. Oh, hello. Fancy meeting..." *And all that.*

"I was speeding, Officer," Molly interrupted. "I'll take my ticket now."

"I'm almost there!" Marla screamed from the cell in Mitzi's lap which somehow was now on speakerphone. "Where in the freak are you people! Oh crap, I see Mom's car."

Mitzi snapped her phone shut and grinned. "Another sister."

"Hm."

"I don't usually speed like that, but our mother, she is in a pickle at our grandmother's house and—"

He glared at her. "Driver's license, registration, and proof of insurance, please."

"Oh, of course." Molly leaned to pull open the glove box.

"Find the registration and insurance for me, okay Mitz? I'll get my license."

"Be quick about it," Mitzi whispered.

Finally, they retrieved the documents and handed them to Officer Dryden. He nodded and stepped back to his cruiser and sat.

"I want to say that F word."

"Say freak."

"It doesn't pack as much punch."

"I know. But we don't want to get charged for cursing in front of an officer."

Mitzi scowled. "Is that really a thing?"

Her phone rang again. She pushed the button. Still on speaker. "Why did you cut me off?"

"Marla, go in and distract Mom for a moment. We've got, um, a police situation here."

"F—"

"Don't say it."

"Ahem." Dryden was back in the window. Mitzi hit the soft key on her phone to set it to vibrate.

"Mrs. Campbell?"

"Yes?" The eye batting again.

He handed her back her documents and pulled out his pad of tickets. "Stop sign. You ran it. Big mistake. Fifty miles per hour in a 25-mph zone. Bigger mistake." He finished writing, tore off the ticket, and handed it to her, just out of her reach. "What's the rush?"

"Well, you see, our Mom is at our Gran's house and—"

"She's not feeling well, Officer, and was upset when she heard about the shooting, and...."

"I see." Again, he looked long and hard at Mitzi. He pushed the ticket closer, and Molly grasped it. "I have your cell phone number from the police report, Ms. Winston. I'll be in touch this evening."

"Oh, sure, fine."

He tipped his hat then left.

"Wait!" she yelled, leaning over to Molly's side.

The officer took a slow turn and reversed a few steps. One eyebrow cocked at her. "Yes?"

"Can't tonight. I have a party."

The eyebrow straight-lined and joined the other one. "Of course, a party always takes precedence over a police matter."

"It does when the party is for your daddy."

He eyed her, long and steady, for about the lengthiest ten seconds Mitzi thought she'd ever live through. "Tomorrow. I'll call you tomorrow."

"Thank you." He left then. Finally.

Both sisters breathed a long sigh.

"I don't like him," Molly said.

"Ditto."

* * *

Seven minutes later Molly and Mitzi burst through the door of their Gran's house only to find no one on the main floor or upstairs.

"Marla's Honda is outside and Mom's Bonneville, too. Where are they?" Mitzi stood on the second-floor landing and asked the question out loud.

"I don't know. I got here same as you!"

They ran downstairs and into the kitchen then burst onto the sun porch at the back of the house.

Marla and their mother glanced up from where they were having tea. It was quite a serene situation to be certain and conflicted greatly with Mitzi's frantic mood of the moment.

She hated that.

Marla smiled faintly and gave her sisters a little finger wave. "Mom! Marla?"

Their mother, sitting prim and ladylike on a wicker chair carefully placed her china teacup back on its saucer. Marla sported a sheepish look from the other side. "Well, my goodness. All my girls in one place. A rare occasion, to be sure. Why, sit down, sweets, and I'll put on some more hot water. It's been way too long since we've sipped tea from Gran's bone china."

She rose with Southern grace and charming elegance, her floral, decades-old Gloria Vanderbilt wrap dress falling into place as she stood and smiled at her daughters. Her pedicure was new, as were her sandals, Mitzi was certain. And likely, since it was Saturday, her mother had just come from the hairdresser, her still-brunette doo coifed and fluffed. Lucky for her, big hair was making a comeback.

But wait. This was the South. Big hair reigned.

"Molly, you look lovely." She smiled at her youngest then focused on Mitzi. "Oh dear, honey? Have you been having a bad day? You look, well, rather a fright."

A ghostly fright was more like it.

Sighing and ready to collapse in one of Gran's wicker chairs sporting bright striped cushions, Mitzi felt deflated. Why did her mother always do that to her? "Well, hell yes, Mother, I've had quite the morning." She waved her off then, not really wanting to get into any conversation that had to do with estranged husbands, ghosts, and drive-by shootings. So, she just sat. "But fiddlededee, that is none of your concern. Got any Earl Grey?"

Priscilla Newberry smiled and touched Mitzi's cheek in that knowing way that mothers do. "Of course. Just relax, and I'll be right back."

She left, and Molly fell into a chair, too. "I feel like I've been wrung through a ringer washer."

"You?" Mitzi grabbed a piece of biscotti, "I'm the one who looks a fright, now." She tugged the cookie out from where it lay nestled amidst a couple of scones on a green Depression-era plate in the center of the glass-topped wicker table. She took an odd look at it and then bit. Crunch. "Only our mother would bring biscotti and scones, and wear a Sunday dress, to clean house."

"Oh, she's not really cleaning. A maid service is due here any sec," Marla replied.

"Of course."

The sisters glanced from one to another.

"Has she been in the basement?" Mitzi took another bite and grimaced.

"Don't think so." Marla sipped her Earl Grey. Or perhaps it was Constant Comfort. More her style.

"Good. We have to keep her out. The maids, too."

Marla reached for a scone and broke one in half. "What are scones, anyway? Biscuits or bread?"

"Who cares?" Mitzi was getting aggravated. Their mother was taking her sweet time and she was antsy. "Shit, the maids. Forgot about them. Who's going to be around? I can't stand watch all day."

Molly picked at the other half of Marla's scone. "Well, I certainly can't. For one I have appointments, and for another I'm not dressed for it."

"Hell's bells, Molly. If mom can point her finger in her floral designer dress, you can do it in your lavender suit. Reschedule!"

Molly looked at Mitzi. "Well, he's your ghost-hubby, my dear sister. I would think Dead Ken is like, your responsibility, correctomundo?"

"I don't care who does it as long as we keep them all away from the basement," Mitzi said.

"Yeah, we can't have anyone down there sniffing around the stiff."

Priscilla breezed into the room on the heels of Marla's words.

"Stiff? What's stiff?"

Molly sat up straighter. "Um."

"Stiff. Crisp. The biscotti, Mom. It's really nice and dry and stiff today." Mitzi smiled and took another bite. "You make these?"

Her mother bore a tray filled with two more china teacups and a few added pieces of biscotti. She scoffed, "Oh, pshaw, Heaven's no. Tastes like stale bread to me. I don't know why people rave about biscotti so. You know it's all the rage down at the Coffee Caper. Harriett Adams just got a contract with them to supply them with fresh biscotti every other day. The word! Fresh biscotti? I didn't think there was such a thing. There's a term for that, isn't there? I think it's oxycotin or something."

"Oxymoron."

"Yes. That's right. Fresh biscotti is an oxymoron. I'll have to remember that."

"They'll love that down at the Coffee Caper, Mom." Mitzi stood.

"You're a moron," Marla teased.

A brassy ring pealed throughout the house like a carousel ride run amok. Gran's broken doorbell. Had been that way since '69.

"Ah, the maids." Priscilla flipped out a hand. "I'll get it."

In a cloud of perfume and swishing floral fabric, she left them. As soon as she was out of earshot, Mitzi waved her sisters closer, and they leaned over the table.

"All right. We need a plan. Here's what I'm thinking. The

main objective is to keep everyone out of the basement. Especially Mom, but of course, the maids, too. One of us has to take up post in the kitchen near the basement door at all times."

"I can do that," Molly volunteered.

Mitzi was skeptical. "I dunno, Mol. Can you intercept and decoy in that lavender suit?" She wondered how forceful her sister could get if the going got rough.

Molly's eyes grew big. "You always think I can't do my part." She stood and tugged down her waist-length jacket. "I'm here to tell you, I can do this job."

Mitzi glanced at Marla, who nodded. "Let her do it."

Hells freakin' bells. "All right."

Molly sat back down, a smug grin across her face.

"I'll run interference upstairs," Marla said. "I can keep the maids busy for hours up there with all those nooks and crannies. I'm sure there are dust bunnies galore. And we all know that Gran wasn't the best housekeeper."

Mitzi thought about that. "Okay. So. Then that leaves...."

"Mom," all three sisters chimed at once.

Crap. "Okay, I've got Mom."

Chapter Eight

"Mom?"

Priscilla floated through the door with a saccharin smile. "Well, that task is done," she told them. "I started two of them upstairs, and the little dark-haired one, I think she must be Mexican or something, in the downstairs bath." She paused and glanced off. "I suppose she's Mexican, although she said, 'Hello, Ma'am,' rather than *hola*. Mexicans say *hola*, right? Anyway, she looks Mexican, like that explorer girl on the cartoons, you know?"

Mitzi looked to her younger sister, cringing at her mother's lack of PC—Political Correctness. "Mom, you aren't making sense. And please do not say things like that out in public."

Priscilla arched a brow. "Why?"

"Dora-the-Exploraaaa," Molly explained. She has a three-year-old.

"Oh."

"Well, anyway, I started the girl in the downstairs bathroom which is a good thing. It will keep them out off the kitchen while I'm making the blackberry cobbler for your daddy's birthday cake."

The sisters exchanged glances. Mitzi's heart did a double-half-gainer-triple-backflip.

"Blackberries?"

Molly rose. "Blackberry cobbler is not cake, Mother. I'm sure Daddy will want cake."

"No. He specifically ordered blackberry cobbler. We have all those blackberries in the freezer, you know, Marla? And he loves the stuff even though the seeds give him the runs for a couple of days after."

All three sisters grimaced.

"It wouldn't be so bad, actually, if it weren't for his hemorrhoids."

"TMI, Mother."

"Ewe."

"Not thinking about that."

Marla stepped beside Molly. Mitzi watched her sister clutch Molly's hand at her side. "No, not the blackberries, Mom. I was...I mean, I picked those, and I have plans for them...was going to make jam for jam cake for this winter. Christmas gifts. Please don't use my blackberries, okay?"

Marla was lying through her teeth.

Their mother rotated toward the kitchen door. "Oh fiddled-edee. There are plenty down there for jam and whatnot. When-ever did you start baking anyway? Besides, I already took some from the freezer." She stopped and glanced over her shoulder. One manicured hand rested on the doorframe. "They are thawing in the refrigerator."

Three gasps went up behind her.

"Molly," she drawled, "that was a mighty big deer Don shot last fall, wasn't it? Damn thing nearly took up all of Gran's freezer space. It was all I could do to get three bags of blackber-ries out. When does he plan to cut the rest of that thing up?"

Mitzi knew at that point, if she could pan out of herself, like in one of those out-of-body experiences, and look at her and her sisters all at the same time, they each would have the same oh-freakin'-crap expression on their faces. For a moment, she felt she did have that strange out-of-body thing going on because she wasn't quite certain her heart had not skipped a dozen beats or two or more.

She might just join Ken in his deadliness any second.

"Um. Deer?"

Priscilla's heels clicked off on the wooden floor and into the kitchen. "Yes," she called out. "And he must have left the head on, too. I could see an antler poking up. Strange," she muttered while pulling out pots and pans and slapping them on the counter. "I could swear they were supposed to take the head off and cut the whole animal up before freezing it, but what do I know I leave those things to the men."

The only thing Mitzi could do at that moment was close her eyes and practice deep breathing. She did that for, oh, about six breaths then opened her eyes and looked at her siblings.

Their wide-eyed stares met her back.

Her next words hissed through her teeth. "No one, and I repeat, no one, leaves that freakin' kitchen until she's gone."

On an exhale, she lifted her gaze to the clock on the wall over her mother's head. Exhausted, she sighed. A quarter past two. *My how time flies when you're having a nervous breakdown.*

* * *

They tucked their mother into her Bonneville a little under two hours later. The birthday cobbler sat cooling on the kitchen counter. The cleaning crew, along with the sisters, made short work of tidying up the house. Mitzi put a padlock on the basement door and made sure the door behind her locked as she exited the porch.

The silver sedan backed out of the drive, and her mother shouted from the road, "Don't forget the ice cream. See you at six! No, make that five-thirty!"

Mitzi puffed out her cheeks and blew out a breath. "Ice cream, schmice cream. I got a dead body in the freezer, and we're going to have a party. How many people are coming?" She smiled sweetly and waved back to her mother.

"All of us, the Bransons, the St. Andres, and the new preacher and his wife." Us meant all the immediate family, including Molly and her hubby and three munchkins.

"The preacher, huh?"

"Yeah. Mom invited them last week after service."

"Figures. She's always trying to save Daddy."

"Like Daddy needs saving. He's the most perfect man I know." Molly's gaze followed their mother's car down the street.

"All little girls think their daddy is perfect," Marla said.

"Well, I'm grown up, and I still think he's perfect."

Mitzi plunged ahead. "So, you don't believe that thing about him and one of the secretaries down at the Water Board?"

Molly gasped. "What?"

Marla snickered.

Mitzi continued. "I suppose it's just a rumor." Then grinning, she added, "Don't have a hissy, Molly, I was just pullin' your leg. Of course, Daddy is perfect." She frowned. She had heard that rumor, but she guessed Molly hadn't, so she'd just let the girl live in her perfect world. "Still doesn't explain Mom inviting the new preacher though." Hm. What had her daddy done? The preacher only comes to visit when Mom feels he needs to repent.

Well, she supposed that was their business, and none of their children's. If there was one thing she'd learned over the years, it was to stay out of her mother and father's personal life.

Besides, she had bigger fish to fry.

Huffing out a breath, she spurted out. "I must get home. I need to take care of a few errands before the party. Am I bringing the ice cream or one of you?"

"Can one of you please? It will be all I can do to get my evil children ready on time to get here."

Marla volunteered, and Mitzi was grateful. One less thing.

* * *

At long last, Mitzi eased into her shower and relished the stinging hot stream pelting her back. It felt like hours since she'd woken and even longer since she'd had a good soak. What was it, yesterday? Hell, it was nearly four in the afternoon, and the day had seemed like, oh, seven weeks long already.

Mentally, she ticked off the events of the past seventeenish hours. She'd almost gotten a job, encountered her estranged hubby, found him lying dead on the floor in a halo of blood, spoken to his ghost, moved his body, gotten shot at, tangled with the police more than once, kissed her ghostly ex-hubby, and stashed him away in her Gran's freezer with the blackberries.

Not a bad *less than a day's* work, huh?

No wonder she was dead tired.

Dead.

Ken was dead.

She had to stop using that word so casually. Now that she knew exactly where Ken was—and that he was deceased—the word took on an entirely different meaning.

Her brain spun under the steady stream of water. What would she do? How in the world would she get out of this mess?

She weighed her dilemma and her options.

Ken couldn't stay in the freezer forever. It was too nerve-wracking thinking someone would find him.

And he couldn't hover around for the rest of her life. Or his life. No, he didn't have a life anymore, did he? Or, maybe he had an afterlife? So where was he now? How can he appear and disappear? Maybe, like she's seen on some of those TV shows with mediums, he hasn't crossed over yet and is restless.

Maybe it's *her* job to help him cross over?

Maybe he has a job left undone?

Maybe...both?

"That's it!" Mitzi snapped her fingers. Of course, her fingertips were prunes, so the snap was less than satisfying. "Ken has left something undone. What is it?" And could it have something to do with her? And *was* she supposed to help him go to the light?

Or, wherever?

"You're smarter than the average bear, you know that Boo Boo?"

"Shit!"

Molly spun under the steaming downpour and ran smack into solid flesh, er, ghostly pseudo-flesh, or something.

Ken. Dammit! "Don't do that!"

"What?"

"Scare me."

"I'm a ghost. Boo."

"Right. Ha. Please stop coming and going. It's annoying."

"Hey, I'm ghost. Ghosts are supposed to be annoying."

"Dammit, Ken."

"I'd rather be coming, however." He snaked a hand about her waist.

"Stop that! Quit sneaking up on me. I'm in the shower!"

"I know. Why do you think I picked this time to annoy you?"

"I have no clue but get out. There is not room enough in here for the two of us."

"Would you rather be in our bed?"

"You mean my bed. It's not been our bed in a long time."

He reached for her. "I know, baby. It's been too long."

She pushed away. "Get out, Ken. I don't need your ghostly self hanging around or your sexual innuendo. Besides, what the hell could you do in our bed anyway? You're a ghost. I'm sure ghosts still don't want it. I'm sure ghosts can't even get..." then she remembered this morning, and as if on cue, he reached for her hand, "it up," and placed it on his oversized, quite erect, and extremely firm-of-flesh organ.

If she were butter, she'd be a puddle on the floor right now. *My but that man's engorged penis in my hands feels so—*

"No!" She backed up as far as she could. "Get out!"

"Ah, c'mon, Mitzi baby. Just a little nuzzle. What a tease you are."

"Me?"

"Yes, you." He glanced about. "See anyone else in this shower?" He pressed her backside up against the shower wall. The spray fell over his left shoulder.

He moved in, and Mitzi thought that his hot, naked, and wet body grazing against hers had never quite felt so good. A strange and welcome tingling started in her center, jack-knifed between her legs, rotated and shot up toward her chest, rolled around over her nipples, then ricocheted back down toward the tips of her toes.

"Oh, Ken. Please don't do this." Her words were less than convincing, she knew.

"Ah, honey." His hands splayed one on either side of her head, the hard plane of him flat against her now. His mouth went to that place right below her ear, the one that he could always make tingle with delight, and he burrowed in.

Licking. Sucking. Raking his lips over that tender spot.

She didn't quite know what to do with her hands.

She wanted to touch him. Really wanted to. But she was trying to get past the scary ick factor, and there she was, wet and naked, with Ken's damn hot body rubbing against hers, warm water raining down on them, and her arms stuck straight out at her sides like a stupid telephone pole.

What to do? What to do?

Ken was dead! But...but...but he was also very much in human form and felt way too damned good, and she'd always been a little tart, as he had reminded her yesterday, and it had been a long time since they had been together.

"You want me baby. I can feel it. Relax."

She closed her eyes. Involuntarily, her arms snaked around his waist, and she ran them over his back.

Ken groaned. "Ah, sweetheart...."

There were a thousand reasons why she shouldn't be doing this, and she ran through all one thousand of them in about six milliseconds. Ken had left her. He stiffed her for money. He'd been gone two years without a word. He had tricked her into coming for the interview. He was dead. *Dead!*

A ghost.

Spirit.

Something, but dead all the same.

Now, his right hand, which had moved between her legs, was driving her frickin' insane with pleasure.

Forget dead. An orgasm was imminent.

And this was her husband.

How could this be wrong?

Chapter Nine

"Oohhh..."

The utterance whooshed out on a panted breath that she'd held for at least two years, she imagined, private time with vibrator notwithstanding. Even then, it was not this intense. Ken's fingers had worked over her little nubbin until he'd cranked her libido to about as high a pitch as she could stand, riveted her over the edge to the point of nuclear melt-down, then brought her down slowly, and certainly, with practiced ease.

He always was good at that.

Her body was liquid. Hot and steamy, the shower did nothing to quell the sultry, I-want-more-sex mood that she was in. His fingering her was only the beginning, and Mitzi knew that. So, without further hesitation, she flung one leg up around his waist and grabbed either side of his head, ghost be damned, to bring his fabulous lips to her mouth and his cock to her crotch.

"Oh, hell, Mitz..."

Ken rammed her into the tile, one hand holding up her leg and steadying her against the shower. Mitzi grasped his shoulders as he lifted her slightly and brought her body up to meet his. With a grunt and a shudder, Ken pushed forward and that phallus that she'd joked about earlier impaled her with purpose and need.

God, he felt good. Filling her. Sliding in and out of her. Grinding against her.

Ken raised her leg higher, gaining better access and driving deeper into her body.

"Goddamn..." Ken said. "Honey, it's been too long."

"Yes, yes..."

A twittering of passion raced up to her chest and back again to her pussy. Her clit tingled with need, craving another over-the-top orgasm. Ken ground and pumped, and she held on as the warm water splayed over his back.

"K-Ken..."

He groaned. "Ah, fuck..." he said, drawing out the nasty word. She liked it when he said naughty words.

"Oh, God, I want to come again...."

Ken pulled away, removed himself from her body and stepped back a half step.

"Wha—"

"Hold on, baby."

His hands splayed over her body, and he knelt before her. Spreading her legs wide, he lifted one thigh slightly and held it up against the shower wall. With the other, he spread the wet curly hairs over her clit and burrowed in with his tongue.

Mitzi cried out. "Ken!"

The touch of his tongue to that particular piece of her flesh never failed to send her spiraling into an orgasmic abyss. Within seconds, as the pointed tip tickled and played, the orgasmic craving that was standing alert on the very edge of that small piece of flesh and nerve-endings, exploded into raw and untainted bursts of pleasure.

And again.

Rolling.

Over her body like rogue waves crashing to the shore.

It took a moment for her to come back to earth and all the while that was happening, Ken had turned off the shower, scooped her into his arms, and carried her to their bed where he wasted no time in covering her body with his, penetrating her with his massive and long-in-need pointy thing, and making sweet and bad and sexy and raunchy and intimate love to her.

Not once.

Not twice.

But at least three times.

And when Mitzi woke sometime later from her nap, rolling over to nuzzle into Ken's side, she found out that, a) Ken was not there (was he ever?) and, b) the time was now fifteen minutes until six.

In one motion she flung the covers off and bolted from her bed. "Shit!"

* * *

The party was in full swing by the time Mitzi got there. It had taken a full five minutes for her to semi-fix her hair, from where it had dried and matted against her face from sleeping in wet-shower-hair after making delicious and earth-shattering love to Ken all afternoon. Then another ten to find something half-way decent to wear (she'd not done laundry much lately) and another full ten to drive to Gran's house. She hadn't wanted to risk getting pulled over by Dryden again. The guy gave her the creeps.

She gripped the steering wheel tight as she looked up to her Gran's house, the lights all ablaze, and bodies filtering in and out from behind the windows. Sighing deep, she sat in her car and stared ahead, suddenly in a quandary as to what to do next.

Her daddy expected her at the party, and yes, she damned well had better make an appearance, but there were just too many other things pressing that needed attention.

The shooting was one of those. Who had shot at her?

And Dryden. What did he want? Or, better yet, what did he *know?*

And Ken. WTF? Where had he gone after they'd made love?

She had half a mind to charge downstairs to the basement and ream him a new one. Cold, dead, bastard. Just like Ken, love her and leave her.

In death we do part.

Son. Of. A. Bitch.

And, she'd had to go and let him touch her, please her, and penetrate her with his goodies.

What was she going to do? She couldn't deny that Ken had aroused more than her libido this afternoon, he had gotten to her emotionally, as well. She was, *damn*, having *feelings* for him. And not bad ones, but good ones. Like, that she missed him and wanted him back.

Feelings of something like love, maybe.

But this was impossible. He was dead.

Shit. He was going to make her mourn him. Holy. Shit. All this time that he'd been gone, and she'd come to grips with the fact that he was never coming back, and now...now this. Now he was back, even though he was dead, and had made her fall in love with him all over again.

Blah-freakin'-crap. What the hell?

"Just go to the party, Mitzi," she muttered while jerking the keys from the ignition. She slipped them into her jeans pocket (knowing that her mother was going to give her a look for wearing jeans to her daddy's party, but what the hell, it wasn't like she had a lot of time to primp now, was it?) as she left the car and slammed the door shut. Thank goodness she was the last one here. She got the prime spot in the driveway (the one with exit privileges).

Last in line, first to leave.

Well, at least one thing was going her way this day.

* * *

"Mitzi!"

Lou Sparkles. Great.

The squeal came up from across the room as soon as she slipped inside the door to the front room. Now everyone knew she was making a grand, if not late, entrance. So much for the lie she'd formed in her head while walking up the porch steps about telling her mother she'd been here all along but was helping Molly with her kids. Molly always needed help with her kids.

While one had to potty, the other needed a drink, and the third needed to stop crying—while the first then needed wiped, and the second one had now spilled her milk on her dress, which made the baby cry again even harder because the middle child had spewed chunks after the spilt milk...

And on it went.

But now, Lou Sparkles was scuffing across Gran's Oriental carpet in too high heels, sort of hunched over and grinning like a silly hyena, and sloshing droplets of pink punch over the sides (her mother would have a fit about that later) of her pressed glass punch cup.

Now, Lou Sparkles wasn't Mitzi's best friend or anything close, but there were times, like in social situations when it was to her benefit, when Lou made out that they were. Mitzi was sure this was going to be one of those times.

Marla stepped up next to Mitzi and snickered. "BFF Lou, two o'clock. Danger, Will Robinson. Danger."

Mitzi rolled her eyes. "Save me."

Lou leaped the last two steps and gave Mitzi a huge Southern Belle-like bear hug. Marla wrangled the grape-leafed punch cup from Lou's hands.

"Sparkles!" Mitzi greeted the woman back.

Now, the woman's name wasn't really Sparkles. Her last name was Sparks. But ever since Mitzi could remember, everyone had called her Sparkles because of her sickening sweet, holier-than-thou, sparkles and light, countenance. She was several years older than Mitzi, even older than Marla, but she continued to dress like a twenty-something and had pretty much alienated every woman in two counties with her effervescent BFFishness.

Not to mention there wasn't a man in those two counties who would touch her with a ten-foot pole.

In short, she was a sparkly spinster, which wasn't a pretty thing in small Southern towns, and it was always best, if one could, to avoid Lou Sparkles like the plague.

Lou linked her arm at Mitzi's elbow and squealed again. "What a great party!" She glanced from Marla to Mitzi. "I'm so glad I could come. Why, your daddy has been so excited about this all week. You know we're tight, huh? I mean, I kept telling him that surely you girls were going to have a surprise party for him! I mean everyone down at the water board..."

Mitzi peeled Lou from her arm. "Oh, Sparkles... Well, about that. It's not really a surprise. Daddy knows."

She waved a hand in the air. "Oh, I know! He already told me that, too!"

Liar.

Sparkles glanced off and sighed, taking in the crowd. Mitzi leaned back and looked at her sister behind Lou's back. She arched a brow, and Marla just shrugged.

No. They were not thinking the same thing, were they?

The rumor around town? About their Daddy and a woman at the plant board?

No. Nooooooo....

Again, Sparkles hefted a sigh. Mitzi looked at her straight on. Lou hugged a little closer to her and said, "This is all so very cool, Mitzi dear. I mean, it's kind of like we're sisters, you know? Like I'm a part of the family. Your Gran's house is just so nice, and I feel so comfortable here and..."

Again, Mitzi peeled herself from the clinger. "Sparkles, look. Quit putting a bead on our Gran's house and her things. And our daddy. Now." She faced her and grabbed Marla's arm at the same time. "We have to go help our *mother* get our *daddy's*, birthday cake, er, cobbler, ready, so I suggest that you..."

"Oooh! I'll help!" Sparkles squealed, so not taking the hint.

The only thing Mitzi could think of to do was thrust the stupid woman at her sister. Marla stepped back and steadied the woman. "Intercept! Now!" Mitzi growled out and turned to find their daddy, right this instant.

She was going to put this rumor to bed once and for all.

But she didn't get very far because a brisk knock came at the door behind her. She swiveled around about the time her Aunt Sophie opened it and in stepped Dryden. The party-pooper. And then, almost simultaneously, Ken nuzzled up behind her and whispered in her ear.

"Time to go, Mitz," he whispered. "Get the hell out of here. And while you are at it, get my body out of the freezer and back to the office on Halifax Street. I don't care how you do it, but do it now, and do it fast. Both our futures depend on it."

Whirling again, she looked to find Ken gone, her gaze,

rather, falling on Sparkles being bicep-held from behind by Marla, while her sister Molly stood staring from her left with the baby perched on her hip, her mother peeking in from the kitchen door and carrying the blackberry birthday cobbler, and her father exiting the guest bathroom under the stairs while hitching up his pants and checking his fly.

"Ms. Winston," the voice from the door said. With a snail's pace turn, she rotated back to look at Dryden, while the party around her gradually hushed and silenced.

"Yes?"

"I'm afraid I need to speak to you, Ma'am. It has to do with the shooting at your house this morning and a person of interest."

"Shooting!" Her mother gasped and the blackberry birthday cobbler crashed to the floor.

"What the hell?" Her father shouted.

"Oh! Drama!" Sparkles twittered. "I love drama!"

"Shut her the f—"

"Got it." Marla wrestled Sparkles backwards.

"Officer, of course. I'll be right there. I'm coming. Just one sec..." The last thing she wanted was Dryden inside the house, so Mitzi figured the porch was the best bet. But she needed a moment to think because her brain had become all befuddled since making love with Ghost Ken this afternoon and now all this crap with Sparkles and her daddy, and what *had* Ken whispered in her ear just now? Something about *getting out*? And *moving his body*?

So...

"If you'll wait outside for me, I'll be right there, Officer. Let me help my mother clean up this mess." She gave him a slight smile (on the inside, however, she wasn't smiling). "And calm her down just a stitch or two."

The officer nodded and went to the porch. Thank God for

small miracles. Remind her to tithe a bit more at church on Sunday. Aunt Sophie closed the door. The room erupted with a collective outpouring of questions.

Get out. Get out now.

Ken.

Move, I tell you. Move it and do as I say. Do not trust Dryden. Get my body and get the hell out. Now!

She'd never felt such a strong will to obey Ken in all their married days. That "obey" thing in the vows had never set well with her. Good thing she wasn't Southern Baptist. But for some odd reason, all she wanted to do was exactly what Ken demanded of her at this moment. So, with Dryden waiting for her on the front porch, her mother staring aghast at the floor in the kitchen, her sister still holding back Sparkles who was edging all goo-goo eyed toward their daddy, and all the other chaotic mess of questions and innuendo flying about, she did the only thing she knew how to do.

Take charge.

She bounced her gaze from her immediate family, to the Reverend and his wife, the St. Andres, the Bransons, back to her Aunt Sophie, then on to Molly's husband, Don, and her two nieces and one nephew and said, "There is no need for panic here." Why she felt the need to explain all this, she did not know, but that was what she was doing. "Yes, mother, there was a shooting, but as you can see, I'm fine. Yes, there have been some things going on, but I'm about to fix that." She glanced about. "I need for all of you to trust me on this, y'all here? You all stay put and have a party. *I mean it!* Do not go on the porch, don't talk to that officer out there, don't let on like I am not here, and do *not*, whatever you *do*, go *in the basement*. Do you *hear* me?"

They all nodded, shell-shocked looks on their faces, and Mitzi, for once, was glad that she had taken ROTC classes in college and learned how to bark orders. She was, after all, the best drill sergeant ever at Wellesley Presbyterian College. They were all under her command, and to hell with anyone who crossed the friggin' line.

Her last order was this: "Molly! Marla! To the basement. Pronto!"

Chapter Ten

"Oh, God. Oh, *God!*"

"I can't believe we are doing this."

"Just shut up, okay? And be thankful that it's raining."

Molly jumped on that one. "Why in hell would I be thankful that it is raining? My hair is ruined, my Jimmy pumps are soaked, and I hate thunder!"

Mitzi shook her head and momentarily closed her eyes. "Never mind." She nodded to Marla, who was peering backwards out the driver's side window of Molly's lavender caddy, squinting in the rain. "Back it up. Closer." She gave Marla a motioning signal. "There. Now. Good."

She put up a hand to halt.

Molly bit her lip. "Oh, God. Oh, God! I can't believe we are doing this, *again!*"

Mitzi ignored her. Marla got out of the car. "We don't have a lot of time to hash this out, okay?" She eyeballed her two sisters. "Dryden is on the porch, and that's a good thing, he can't see us at the back of the house down over the hill. I'm pretty sure the storm has kept him there, rather than heading out to his cruiser.

We sure don't want to give him a heads up that I'm leaving. And I think that he won't suspect that it is me leaving in the caddy when he sees you, Molly, driving out of here."

"But why are we doing this? I don't understand."

"Because Ken told me to leave, to get his body out of here, and he said not to trust Dryden."

"So, like," Marla began, "you're taking orders from Ken now? When did you ever take orders from Ken?"

"Ever since he said it would affect my future. All right? I want a future. I'm moving the corpse." Besides, he really said *our future,* and she wanted to know exactly what he meant by that.

Molly's lips trembled. "But I can't leave? What about my kids? And Don?"

"I'll handle it," Marla said. "We'll call him once we're on the road. You won't have to talk to him."

The younger sister nodded her head in agreement. "Good. Sometimes he gets so mad at me, and I don't have a clue why. He tells me I don't have the brains God gave a goose."

Mitzi, while moving toward the basement back door, halted a second. That was the second time lately that Molly had mentioned something weird about Don, and that bothered her. Molly was certainly a ditz at times, but she didn't deserve to be called a Goose-brain.

Shaking that off, she unpadlocked the old back door. "Thank God I remembered where Gran hid this key."

The basement door swung inside and the sisters all moved into the cellar and headed toward the freezer. Marla reached up to pull the switch on the one hanging light bulb in the center of the room.

"Don't turn that on! I don't want anyone to see, in case they get curious!" Mitzi panicked.

Marla countered. "Like a lavender Cadillac backed up

against the cellar door isn't a clue? C'mon. We need to move fast. The light will help us get in and out of here a lot quicker."

Mitzi reneged. "All right." She raced to the freezer. "Let's just get the stiff and go."

She lifted the lid, and all three sisters peered inside.

And gasped.

No Ken.

"Shit. Shit!" Mitzi swirled, her gaze travelling over every inch of the basement. "Where the fuck is he?"

"I can't believe you said that word."

"Oh, Molly, get over it."

At this moment, her panic button was pretty much pushed to the max. She didn't know how much more she could take. The F-word was the least of her problems. *Ken, where are you?*

"Ahem."

Mitzi spun to her rear. There Ken stood, beside the stairwell, pointing to a tarp-encased something on the floor.

"Oh, shit. He's out! How did he get out?"

Marla raced to where Mitzi pointed.

"Can we just get Dead Ken out of here and get back to our normally scheduled lives?" Molly whined.

"I would so like that, too, sweetheart," Ghost Ken muttered. Mitzi looked at him with a pang of hurt. *Oh hell, Ken, I do love you, you bastard. I wish things had been different....*

He nodded and smiled, like he understood.

"I wonder how long he's been out of the freezer?" Marla looked down at him.

"Just about twenty minutes," Ken interjected. Mitzi lifted her gaze, and he shrugged. "Why do you think I came and got you? Your dad took me out to put in the ice cream. I think his hernia is back, by the way. But he affectionately kept calling me dear, so I forgave him for dropping me on my pointy thing. Sorta."

She knew her sisters couldn't see or hear him. "Someone moved him. Crap. Dad?" She lifted the freezer lid. "Yep. Ice cream." She whipped her head toward her sister. "Didn't you get the ice cream? Who brought it down here?"

"Well, I gave it to Daddy, but I didn't think...."

"Cripes, Mar."

"Well, it's done now," Marla glanced about. "There's a dolly. Let's use that to get him to the door. He's going to be heavier now that he's frozen."

"Slightly thawed," Ken added.

"Sure thing."

The sisters took to their work. Molly pinched her nose while lifting the feet end of their tarped bundle and rolling him toward the dolly. Mitzi lifted the head end and Marla scooped him up on the two-wheeled thing.

"Okay, to the trunk. Molly, pop it."

"You have the keys, Mar. You backed up it."

Marla steadied the dolly. "Crap. You're right. Mitzi, reach in my pocket and..."

Mitzi watched as Ken stepped up behind Marla who was struggling with steadying the dolly, reached into her pocket, fished out her keys, and gave Mitzi a wink in the process. One corner of his mouth turned up as the keys floated toward Molly.

Mitzi snatched them up and gave Ken a sneer. "Watch it, Buster," she told him.

"Huh?"

"Oh, I have the keys. There." She popped the trunk. Marla pushed the dolly, and the women pressed her from behind as they moved up the slight incline toward the trunk of the Caddy.

Marla and Molly forged ahead. Mitzi closed and padlocked the door behind them. A flash of lightning broke through the evening sky, accompanied by a rumble of thunder and an outpouring of rain.

"Yikes!"

The women picked up speed.

Blue lights flashed against the side of the house.

Molly and Marla rolled the corpse into the back of the trunk. Mitzi took one look at the cruiser heading their way and jumped into the trunk.

Marla leaned in, and Mitzi tossed her the keys.

Molly slammed the lid.

And Mitzi huddled next to cold Dead Ken in the trunk of the lavender Caddy and prayed that Marla could either, a) outrun, or b) outsmart, Barney Fife.

* * *

They didn't get very far, perhaps just to the corner of the house, when the vehicle stopped. Mitzi waited and listened.

A car door slammed.

Thunder.

Voices. Not loud. Women.

A man.

A giggle. *Giggle?*

Rain. Pounding on the trunk roof.

Man's voice again.

Another door slammed. Was it this car or another?

The engine revved. A horn beeped a little. And they moved forward.

That was easy.

Too easy.

At this point, Mitzi didn't even want to know. All she wanted to do was lay there in the trunk, skirt any sort of disaster that might be lurking around the corner, and get on with her life.

Whatever that may be.

The few minutes in the trunk were the quietest, and surprisingly, most soothing minutes she'd had in some time. The rolling thrum of the tires on pavement lured her into a simple, peaceful state.

Almost sleeplike.

It never occurred to her, not once, that she should be frightened. That she was lying next to a dead man in the trunk of a car headed back to a dark and spooky place where her husband had been murdered, and that all of that was a tad unusual. And scary.

In fact, that didn't bother her one bit.

After all, he was her dead hubby, and, well, she still loved him.

She did.

She managed to move enough to hit the dial on her watch to illuminate in the dark. Five minutes after six.

Wait. Or was it five minutes after seven?

Had she fixed her watch, or not?

* * *

Some time later the palm of a hand crossed her mouth and a deep voice whispered in her ear. "Sh, love. It's me. Keep quiet. We need to talk."

Ah, Ken.

In her sleep, she nuzzled into him.

"Darling, I need for you to wake up. C'mon now."

Her lids fluttered open. Dark. It was dark. And she was moving.

Trunk. Still in the trunk. How long had she slept?

She glanced at her wrist.

Ken's hand covered it. "No time for that now, sweetheart."

He was lying next to her, and sort of over her, and he felt, well, delicious. She was warm and cozy and the wheels on pavement were soothing and...

Hell, what was she thinking? "Ken, what is it?"

"We don't have much time. And I need to come clean."

That panged her heart. She'd waited a long time for Ken to come clean. To say that she had his undivided attention was an understatement.

"I'm all ears, Ken baby."

"Good."

He paused, and Mitzi realized her eyes were adjusting to the dark. She could see the outline of Ken's face above her. She loved his face, the planes and angles, his high cheekbones, the cute little dimple-cleft in his chin.

Just like Kirk Douglas, her mother used to say.

Sigh.

That was back in the good old days.

"I don't know how much time we have, but there are some things I need you to know, sweetheart."

"Okay." He had put on his stern voice, which meant it was time for her to pay serious attention. "Go on, Ken."

He paused, and for a moment, his lips gently brushed against hers, sending an electric current through her. "Ken," she whispered.

"I'm sorry, love. It's just that..." He choked up for a second, didn't go on.

"Ken?"

After clearing his throat, he said, "I love you, Mitz. Always have. Always will. None of this was planned. None of it. I have to come clean now so you will know and not hate me for the rest of your life. Because my life, I'm sure, is at the end, seeing that I'm, well, already dead. I wish there was something I could do to alter time, to change the course of events for the past two years, but I can't, Mitzi, and I fear that before long, I won't be here at all anymore. It's strange, I'm somewhat in limbo about my place right now, but I'm feeling compelled to move on, in one direction or the other."

"What does that mean?"

"I'm not totally sure."

"Like, to the light?"

At first he didn't say anything. "Yes. Maybe. I don't know. It's like, well, it's like some higher power out there is telling me to make a decision and be quick about it. All I know is that the first thing I must do is come clean with you."

Suddenly, she didn't want him to leave. "Tell me, Ken. All of it."

His arms wrapped her into a cocoon of warmth as he gathered her close. She didn't want to leave this, really, which was extremely weird and demented seeing that she was in the trunk of a lavender Cadillac lying next to a corpse headed for that icky place at the top of the stairs on Halifax.

"It was the horses."

She knew it. The damn horses. "Go on."

"I got in over my head with the bookies. Too much money. They were after me and then threatening you. I had to do something, love, so I went to the police."

The car hit a speed bump, or something, and they lurched upward.

"Ow!"

"Sh." He covered her mouth with his palm and the touch felt so nice. "Let me get this out, Mitz. I became an informant for the police. I got in deep. And the guys, the family, they were coming after me. And you. But I managed to work enough with the cops so that they got the big guys. All of them. Except for one of the little brothers. We thought he was pretty harmless, until a few days ago."

"And what happened then?" Some things were clicking into place for her.

"I came out from under."

"What?"

"I was in protection. I couldn't tell you, anyone."

"You son of a bitch!"

"Mitzi, I couldn't. They wouldn't let me. I tried, I fought them, they kept me under wraps so tight I could barely piss without an audience. Then they decided they wanted the little brother, too, because he was making waves. And he was talking about coming after you."

"The gunshots?"

"Yeah, I think."

"I convinced them to let me come out as a decoy, to pull the attention away from you to me. And I had a plan, but things were slightly altered last night. See, I was going to steal you away, take you back with me where I could protect you, watch you, while the cops went after Little Joey, the brother. But you showed up late, and then...."

"And then you were dead," she whispered. A shiver raced up through her body and settled in her throat. "Oh, God, Ken. I'm so sorry." Damn her frickin' lazy not-changing-her-clock ways!

He hugged her tight, and that comforted her. Somewhat.

"What do we do now?"

"I wish I knew."

"But you told me to take the body back. Something told you that we needed to do that, right?"

"Yes."

"And Dryden fits into this somewhere, doesn't he?"

He nodded against her chest. His cheek felt warm against her throat. "He snitched to the little brother, I suspect. Dryden never liked me when I was playing informant. Never believed I was telling the truth. I never trusted him then, and I don't trust him now. I think he's taking kickbacks somehow..."

There was a moment of silence, and the car rolled to a stop, the engine still running.

"Think, Ken. We have to think. What do we do now?"

"I guess we go with the plan. Take the body back up. See what happens."

"No."

"No?"

"No. Not before I do this." With everything in her, Mitzi reached for Ken's head and pulled his lips up to hers. She kissed him as mightily, and as thoroughly, as she'd ever kissed him.

"Ah, Mitzi..."

"I just want to say this, Ken. I love you, and I believe you, and I wish like hell you were not dead because I'm already damned missing you and trying to figure out if I need to help you get to the light, or try to find some freakin' way to get you back alive!"

He gasped with pleasure at her statement, and she felt his joy. "Oh, Mitzi. I love you, too, sweetheart. I'm sorry for the gambling, sorry for being such a screw-up, and sorry you've had to deal the past two years without me. I just don't know...."

She put a hand over his mouth. "Enough. We need a plan."

The car moved forward again, rolling slowly down the road.

"Yes. A plan. But wait... Just one more thing to say."

"Go on, Ken."

He sighed. "I keep thinking about the damn time. Twenty-four hours earlier and the outcome might have been different. You and your damned watch. If I could only roll back the clocks. I would. If I could change one thing, one stupid decision I made, then both our lives could be different today. But I can't.

"Mitzi, I'd give anything if I could erase the past two years or even the past twenty-four hours. I just don't know how to do that, and I don't know how to move forward. Maybe if I have your forgiveness, I can at least have that, and my spirit will be at peace."

Ken's words rolled over Mitzi like a steam roller. Or perhaps the better description was like one of those centrifugal force contraptions at the carnival where your body was plastered to the outer wall and spinning around at some ungodly pace.

That's how her head felt at the moment, and all she really wanted to do was take a moment or an hour or another day to ponder it all, but something deep in her gut told her that timing was critical and that acting now or never was the name of the game.

"You know I forgive you, Ken." She had to find a way. They needed a second chance.

Clocks. Time.

You're an hour late, sweetheart, and now I'm dead.

If I could only roll back the clocks. Twenty-four hours.

What time was it now, anyway?

She felt for her watch again. "Ken, what time is it. I need to check the time."

No wait. She hadn't changed her watch yet, had she? Whatever her watch said, it was an hour later than that, right?

He twisted her wrist and lit the dial. "It's seventeen minutes before seven o'clock."

"Wait. No. It's an hour later."

An hour late, sweetheart, and now I'm dead.

"Okay, before eight then." He glanced at the watch again. "Sixteen minutes now."

"Almost twenty-four hours from yesterday when I was supposed to meet you." In fact, it was 23 hours and 44 minutes prior to the time she was to have shown up for her job interview with Ken the day before.

She searched through the dark for Ken's face and thought she saw his eyes flicker.

She loved him. Had always loved him. And this mess he had gotten himself into wasn't entirely his fault, was it? He'd gotten suckered into something, and it spun out of control. His intentions were good. And let's face it, he really didn't deserve to die of that one mistake, did he?

No.

She made a gut decision. Ken deserved to live and they, well, they deserved to find out if they really and truly belonged together. Didn't they?

"Oh, God. We have to turn time back."

"What?"

"The watch. *My watch*! Help me." she yelled, frantically spinning the little dial on the side. It was a long shot but just maybe... "Help me! Take it off, turn the clock back. Because..."

"What are you talking about?"

The car lurched to a stop. Car doors opened and shut. "My watch! You always say I'm late, and I forgot to move the time. You told me it was my fault, remember? I was an hour late because I forgot to change the time. We need to turn it back...twenty-four hours. To before I was supposed to go up there and meet you."

"That was yesterday, Mitzi. This doesn't make sense."

"Set it back twenty-four hours."

"No. No. Twenty-five hours. Right?"

Realization dawned over her. "Yes."

"Will it work?"

"It's worth a try. What do we have to lose?"

They struggled with her watchband, hitting the button at the side to illuminate the clock face. Ken fumbled with it, having a difficult time pulling out the pin.

"I'll do it," Mitzi told him. "Let me."

"Mitzi, stop."

Her gaze lifted to his. "What?"

"Stop for just a minute."

"But I have it. I'm turning it back. Ken! Twenty-five hours. See? I did it. This is going to work."

Tugging her closer, his hands clutched hers. "Are you sure you want to do this?"

She knew that she did. "I don't want you dead, Ken. I want you alive. And I want us to have a second chance. I love you."

"You're sure?"

The trunk latch clicked.

"I'm positive."

Light from a streetlamp flooded the trunk. Ken popped away.

I love you, too.

Chapter Eleven

"So, my dear sister, this is the absolute last time I am hauling this body up, or down, any set of stairs, and the very last time in my lifetime, that I am driving a purple caddy through this side of town after dark."

"It's lavender, Marla."

The older sister rolled her eyes. "Okay, sure, lavender. Fact remains, I'm done with this shit."

Mitzi lifted her hand. "Would you just get me out of here?"

"Whatsamatter, Mitz. Tired of laying with dead guys?"

"Ha." She glanced about. The rain had stopped, but the sky still rumbled. It was darker than a mother-trucker and if she knew anything, it was this—Halifax Street was not the place she truly wanted to hang out on a Saturday night.

But she forgot about all that as soon as she glanced at her wrist. The dial was still lit up. Thirteen minutes until eight o'clock.

She gave a brisk turn toward Ken's body. "Hurry girls, we don't have much time." Tugging on the tarp, the dead-weight body didn't budge much. "Marla! Molly! Chop-chop!"

She turned, and they both just stood there, frozen-like to the spot.

"What the hell?"

Molly's gaze was trained on the second-floor window and Mitzi followed where she looked. The window was open. Broken Venetian blinds skittered in and out on the breeze. "Forget that. If we hurry, we can be done with this, and you can get your caddy back in time to tuck your kiddos into bed."

They stood and looked at her. "Go!"

"Oh, all right!"

"I'm getting really tired of you ordering me around, Mitz."

"Shut-up and grab that end, Marla. This is the most excitement you've had in months. Admit it."

They managed to roll Ken up to the edge of the trunk.

"On three," Mitzi said. Marla was at his feet, Molly the head, and Mitzi, well, she was at the pointy thing.

"Hey, you've got a handle. No fair," Molly said.

"Shut up."

"One. Two. *Three!*"

They hoisted and moved, leaving the trunk open. "Move it girls. Don't stop. Go up the stairs. Deposit the body. And then I want you both to leave."

"Sure thing, Captain. Got a whistle you want me to jump at?"

"Just do it."

They rushed toward the door, awkwardly carrying the corpse. It felt to Mitzi like Ken was getting lighter. Melting? Who knows? They fumbled past the door, up the stairs (and not too quiet about it, truly) and then pushed their way into the room where they'd picked up their Ken delivery earlier in the day.

"There's the spot," said Marla.

"Ewe," came from Molly.

"Set him down and leave."

"Okay." The three placed him on the floor. Mitzi started pulling at the duct tape. "Okay," she said. "Go now." She didn't look at the sisters but did glance at her watch. Nine minutes until eight. "Go now."

"You're coming with us."

She did look up then. "No. No, I'm not. Now, I love you, and if you love me, you will do as I say. Go. Go now. It's for your own safety, and if I play my cards right, my future happiness. Now do as I say and get your freaking asses down that stairwell!"

Her watch said eight minutes of eight.

A brisk wind cut through the open window, scattering pieces of the broken blind.

"Mitzi..."

"Go!"

"All right!"

Her sisters scattered. For a moment, she sat and listened. The trunk slammed. The engine rolled to life. And she heard the caddy speed away.

"How in the world did I pull that off?"

She glanced at Ken. The thing she needed to pull off was the stupid tarp. Ripping, pulling, and breaking the tape with her teeth, she managed to unbind and unroll him and flip the body over to where he was facing up.

She avoided looking at his bloody, meat grinder forehead.

"My, aren't you a sight for sore eyes."

She glanced up. Hadn't heard anyone come up the stairs, but there stood Dryden, his gun leveled at her chest. "Officer?"

"I knew you were in on this somehow," he said, moving slowly toward Ken's feet.

"In on what?"

"His murder."

"Oh, no. Not me. But I did find him. Yesterday. And I..."

"And you're wrapping up the body to dispose of him, aren't you?"

"Oh, no. I'm um, unwrapping him so that..." Hm. How did she say this? So, in case Ken doesn't want to be dead anymore his ghostly form can slip back inside his body and live with her forever?

Somehow she didn't think Dryden was going to buy that.

"Mitzi Winston, you are under arrest."

She stood. "Officer Dryden, you do not understand. I'm not the bad guy here. I'm really trying to do the right thing. I know that you might not totally understand that, and you're really awesome, you know, for investigating every angle and all. It probably does look pretty bad that I'm here standing over a dead body with a tarp and duct tape, but you are a very smart man, and I'm pretty sure you realize, even though the situation looks pretty incriminating, that I'm not your woman. I did not kill my husband." She watched enough Crime TV to know that giving the guy with the gun compliments was usually a good thing.

"That's what they all say."

"Well, this time it's true."

"Not to mention that your sisters just got scared and sped out of here with your getaway car. What are you going to do now, Ms. Winston? Tell me that."

He moved closer, and she looked into his eyes. Something was wrong with this man, she decided. His pupils shifted right and left as if in a nervous twitter. "I...I..."

"Well, well," came a different voice from the door. Dryden didn't move a muscle. Mitzi let her gaze slide past the cop, but it did her no good, she didn't know the man who had just entered.

"Get the hell out of here, Little Joey. I've got the killer right here. You can go free now. Get out of here."

Suddenly it all made sense. Little Joey was Ken's killer.

Dryden was covering for him. Probably so he could keep getting the kickbacks. He was the loser, and she was going to be indicted for the murder of her estranged husband.

Talk about a bad day.

Didn't you hear about stuff like that in the news all the time?

Crap. Ola.

Out of the corner of her eye, she watched Little Joey move further into the room. With her other eye, she held a bead on Dryden. And somewhere in her brain, she registered another presence. Ken?

What to do. What to do?

Little Joey looked down at Ken. "I do good work. Deader than a door nail. But let's just make sure he is really good and dead."

All at once, it sounded to Mitzi as though every ticking clock in the world was echoing in her ears. Tick. Clock. Time.

Little Joey lifted his arm, a pistol in his hand.

She glanced at her watch. The minute hand was almost straight up. One minute until...

Tick. Tick. Tick.

The fuzzy slow motion of the next few seconds would be forever etched in her brain. Little Joey's fingers curled around the trigger; the gun pointed toward Ken's head. Time warped around her as she watched his forefinger twitch on the metal and pull.

Her body took over.

Dryden yelled.

Ken's ghostly vision flashed before her.

She lunged and took out Little Joey, tackling him to the floor. Right as she hit him, the gun went off, shattering the light bulb out in the hallway. They both hit the floor. Little Joey grunted and pushed her away. The gun skittered toward Dryden, who put his foot on it.

Two uniformed officers followed by Marla and Molly burst into the room. The women gasped and screamed. The officers wrestled the struggling and fleeing Little Joey to the floor. But he wasn't going anywhere with Mitzi latched onto his ankles.

She let loose, though, when the officers took over.

Her sisters raced to her side. Mitzi turned back to Ken's body, where he lay face up on the floor. She watched as Ken's ghost spun into a tight orb, then funneled into a misty form, and took a nosedive into his chest.

For a moment, all was silent.

Then Ken coughed, shook and groaned, and rolled toward her to lazily prop himself up on an elbow.

The bloody hole in his forehead was gone.

Excitement and relief flooded through her. It worked, a small voice in her head said, fearful of getting overly excited now. She felt her sisters' fingers clutching her shoulders.

"Well, I'll be shit. Ken's alive," Marla whispered.

"Oh, law, I think I'm gonna puke," Molly echoed.

Dryden droned on in the background. She heard him say something to the officers about him foiling an attempted murder.

Ken sat up and smiled, and Mitzi smiled back.

Epilogue

"You know, it's really a shame that Dryden didn't end up in the same jail cell as Little Joey that night," Mitzi told Ken, several days later.

He looked up from his coffee, gave his morning paper a shake, and slid her a questioning glance. "Why do you say that?"

Laying her palms on the edge of the sink and looking out into her back yard, she replied, "Because Dryden is a weenie, and it would have been nice to think that Little Joey had beat his face to a pulp. Bastard."

Ken chuckled and rose, crossing the distance from the kitchen table to the sink, and stepped up behind her. The warmth he emitted soaked into her back, and all Mitzi wanted to do was stand there and relish the moment.

Thank you, Lord, for giving him back to me.

She didn't know how, or why, it had happened, but she was ever so grateful for the miracle that it was.

He nuzzled behind her right ear with his nose. "That's not a very nice thing to say, Mrs. Winston."

"Well, you didn't like him either."

"I know. The guy is a dick. And a snitch. But Little Joey?

Now, he's brutal. Not sure Dryden would come out of that alive."

She turned into his arms and faced him. Peering up into his face, she whispered, "I sure am glad you are back."

"Ditto."

The phone rang on the counter. Ken smiled and reached for it. "Hello?"

Mitzi could hear a frantic Molly on the other end. A frown crossed Ken's face. "Sure. Okay." He snapped the phone shut.

For a moment, the cat got Mitzi's tongue. Something was wrong. She just didn't know what.

"Tell me."

"That was Molly."

"I know. I heard."

Her brain raced. It was Saturday. Where was everyone? Her daddy should be having coffee down at the Coffee Caper. Her mother? At home in the garden. Marla? Sleeping in no doubt. Molly and the kids and...

Don.

"Something's happened."

He nodded. "Yeah. Don overturned the truck carrying The Grave Dodger on the way to that big truck pull in Athens. Tangled with a semi loaded with watermelon. He's out on Highway 4, just off the Interstate. There was a call from the State Police. It's not good, Mitzi, and Molly needs for you to take her there."

"Oh, shit."

"I'll come with you."

"Gimme the phone."

Mitzi had a gut feeling this wasn't good. Not good at all. She hit Marla's speed-dial button and off they went.

* * *

The End! I hope you enjoyed *Freshly Dead*—I certainly laughed my way through writing it! Care to leave a review? You can do so at your favorite bookstore, or you can leave one on my website. I appreciate and thank you for your feedback! ∼ Maddie

* * *

Get ***Seriously Dead,*** Book 2, right now!
Or scroll on for a sneak peek!

Chapter One—Seriously Dead

"Geez, Molly, do you have to be such a damn needy drama queen?"

Molly Newberry Campbell swiped her nose on her sleeve and looked up at her sisters. She'd just finished a very ugly, hiccupping cry, and had laid her hot, damp cheek flat against the cool lacquered tabletop. The fact that she'd recently downed a little whiskey didn't help. Their corner of the bar was semi-dark, with a smoky haze haloing the lights above them. She squinted first at Marla, her oldest sister, then at Mitzi, the middle sister, and gave them a half-drunk serious stare.

"Actually, yes I do," she slurred. "I just buried my freakin' husband. I deserve needy."

"But we don't need drama queen."

"And it's been two months."

"Plus, you didn't like him much near the end."

"That's not true!" Molly sat up straight in protest, then slid back, planting her face square on the bar.

The youngest Newberry sister, Molly had been babied by the family to some extent—she knew it and didn't deny it. She'd always been coddled, and well, she liked playing the helpless act

107

when she could get away with it. And when they weren't babying her, they generally chided her for her dramatics—but over the past few weeks they had taken super good care of her, and she had no clue how she would repay them.

Tonight, was one of those nights.

"*Only* two months," she reminded, talking into the bar top.

Mitzi sidled up to her. "She's right, Marla. Cut her some slack."

"We were supposed to get her mind off things tonight, not relive them," Marla reminded.

"I love y'all..." Molly drawled, raising up. She took another long sip of her Southern Comfort and ginger ale, fished the Maraschino cherry out with her forefinger, popped it in her mouth and flung the stem away to the floor. Blinking, she stared at her sisters through the brain fog. She wished things were different—but was secretly grateful for the closeness she and her sisters had recently rekindled.

That's what sisters did in a time of crisis. Right?

Even if they were blunt and a little mean girl to her occasionally.

Tragedy. It was all such a tragedy. Everyone said so.

Marla patted the back of her hand. "You know we're here for you, Molly." She shrugged and glanced at Mitzi. "We're always here for each other. Dysfunctional family, or not."

Dysfunctional? She supposed they were. Not every family could say they'd hid a dead body in their Gran's freezer with the blackberries or had witnessed a deceased ex-brother-in-law come back to life in front of their faces.

They were, indeed, unique. That was what one called dysfunctional southern families, right? Yes. They were unique. Sounded a little quirkier and a lot more acceptable put that way.

But as for always being there for each other?

"Well n-not always...." Molly stuttered. "There was that

time that y'all wouldn't bail me out of that blind date with Jimmy Henderson's cousin and I was literally *dying* to get out of the back seat of that old Chevy of Jimmy's at the drive-in over in Athens." She turned to Mitzi. "You remember, don't you Mitz? Gawd. Why do guys think that kissing after eating onion rings is an okay thing?"

"That's a night I'd rather not relive."

Molly hiccupped. "Me neither. Onion ring French kisses are not good."

Mitzi snorted. "That was the night you hooked up with Don, remember? Once we'd snatched you and whisked you away with us to the bowling alley?"

"But not soon enough." She sniffed. "Jimmy's cousin damn near popped my cherry that night."

Marla spit her swallow of beer on the bar. "Shit. I didn't know it was that hot and heavy."

"Not on my end. Thank God you two got there in time. Saved my ass again." She paused, remembering that night and how awful it was at the drive-in. And later, after meeting Don, how the tables had turned. *He was so nice back then.* "Oh, Don..." The sniffling started again.

"Ah, shit, Mitzi," Marla said and elbowed her in her side. "You are an idiot."

Something stabbed Molly straight to the gut. She could do nothing but moan. *Oh, Don...* Mitzi rushed in closer. "I am so sorry Molly. I wasn't thinking. I should have mentioned Don. I'm an insensitive bitch. I...."

"I can't believe he's gone!" Molly shrieked.

Turning heads registered in the periphery of her brain. She was likely about to make a spectacle of herself in one of Carrington, Louisiana's only home-grown pubs. But the locals would understand, wouldn't they? After all, everyone knew Don. Of course, they knew her, too. Or remembered her. She'd been the only double homecoming queen at Carrington High for decades. Both basketball and homecoming. People *knew* her. And *knew* Don. They *were popular*.

No. Prominent, as her mother would say. Popular was for teenagers. Prominent was for townsfolk.

"Oh, my stars! What am I going to do without him, girls? I mean, I have the kids, and the house, and the business and not to mention all those cars and his big-ass trucks and...."

She hiccupped and slugged back the rest of her whiskey. "I am doomed. My life is over. And my poor husband, mangled up in that seven-car pile-up on the interstate. He didn't deserve that."

"Yeah," Marla said. "A semi load of watermelons can sure put a damper on things."

"Good God, Marla!" Mitzi put an arm around her little sister, turning to her. "I know honey. No matter what, Don didn't deserve to die like that. It's going to be tough. You're just lonely now and vulnerable. Things will get better. It's too soon to think that you could get over this so quickly. Give yourself—"

"I hate that bastard husband of mine!"

Marla and Mitzi both jumped back, eyes wide, and Molly almost giggled at their startled faces.

She straightened her back. She might have had one too many whiskeys, but she still enjoyed shocking her sisters. "Well, it's true. Sonofabitch had to go and die. Ripping my life right out from under me. Nasty, belittling, liar of a man. I am more than mad. I am livid!"

And then she broke down and sobbed. "Oh gawd. He's gone. The bastard is really dead. Seriously. Dead."

"Seriously," Marla repeated.

"Dead," said Mitzi.

Molly laid her hot cheek flat against the bar. "Yes. And I'm seriously in a pack of trouble."

Out of the corner of her eye, Molly watched her sisters look at each other, shrug their shoulders, and lean into the table.

"Okay, I'll bite. What kind of trouble, Molly? Spill it," said Marla.

Molly glanced from one sister to another. "Oh, I can't. It's so damn embarrassing."

"Look," Marla said, leaning closer. "You know you're going to have to tell us eventually, because likely we'll be bailing you out, so just go on and say the words."

Molly sucked in a breath and attempted to sit up straighter. "All right."

"Well...?"

"It's money. I have money problems."

"But Don was loaded."

"Was, being the operative word, I guess. Dead guys aren't still loaded."

"But didn't the money go to you? He had insurance, right?" Mitzi peered into her eyes.

Molly shook her head. "Nada. Nothing. No. Apparently not. And it appears he was in debt up to his pretty blue eyeballs."

"Holy shit on a shingle."

"I guess he'd been gambling. There's this guy from the casino who keeps coming by the house to collect."

Marla cocked a brow. "I didn't know Don gambled."

Molly shrugged. "Me, either. Except that he and Tom—you know, his business partner—had been spending a lot of time at the casino lately. Don said it was business, but now I wonder. How many construction deals are made over a blackjack table, really?"

"This is not good, honey." Mitzi bit her lip.

"I know."

"Do you know the guy?"

Molly shook her head. "Never saw him before."

"What did he look like?" Marla edged closer.

Molly sighed. "Tall, bald, tattoo sleeves—looked like he lifted weights."

"Shit." Marla stood. "Okay, we're going to need to find out more information about this guy, who he works for, and what exactly he wants."

Time to fess up, Molly guessed. "Oh, I know what he wants."

Mitzi leaned in. "Spill it, sister."

"Fifty thousand dollars, the Grave Dodger, and to exhume Don's body."

Molly watched both her sisters' eyes grow big, round, and wide, while they jerked up into ramrod straight sitting positions. "What? That's insane."

"That's what I said. Can't get blood out of a turnip, as they say. Stiff bodies, either."

"I mean digging Don back up. Why?"

Molly shrugged. "Make sure he's dead?"

Marla sat down again. "Wow. He is dead. Right?"

"Deader than a doornail. I made sure of that when he was in the casket. I pinched him twice to be sure."

"Good God, Molly."

"Well, I needed to know! He was such a liar. What if he was faking?"

Molly glanced from one sister to the other. Marla still looked shocked and worried about the whole thing. Mitzi seemed to be deep in thought, then she spoke.

"We have to figure out how to get the money to pay this guy off."

Marla drummed her fingers on the slick tabletop. "What about the construction business? What's happening there? Have you spoken with Tom Purdy? I guess you own half of the business now, right?"

"I have no clue. Tom won't return my calls."

Mitzi stood now. "In two months, he hasn't returned your calls?"

"No." Molly shook her head. "I figured he was busy."

"Oh, Jesus take the wheel," Marla exclaimed. "You need help... And this is getting a little weird."

"But you've talked with your attorney, right?" Mitzi stared.

Molly sat silent, watching her sisters' faces.

Marla scooted closer. "Look into my eyes, little sister. You have talked with Jackson Cooper, Don's attorney, right? You have started settling this estate. Correct?"

"Ummm."

"Oh, shit, Molly. What the hell?"

Molly threw up her hands. "I figured I had time!"

"Well, you don't. You need money. And you need to know where you stand with all these financial issues. I'm calling Jackson first thing in the morning and we're getting an appointment."

"No."

"No?"

Molly laid her hand over Marla's on the table. "No. Don't call Jackson. I don't trust him."

"Why?" Marla studied her face.

"Because..." She took a deep breath, then let it out slowly. "Because he cornered me at a party at his house last summer and made a very serious pass at me. Like, tongue in my mouth and hand sneaking up my dress kind of pass. It was gross, like Jimmy Henderson's cousin with the onion rings."

"What the hell?"

"What did you do?"

"Slapped the shit out of him and pushed him off me. He was

drunk, so it wasn't hard. He fell back into a cabinet with glass shelves and broke some expensive knick-knacks. His wife, Grace—you remember her, former Miss Mississippi right?—was furious and yes, we made a scene. Don, the bastard, laughed it off. The next week Jackson came to the house to pay me a visit while Don was at work and told me if I ever tried anything like that again, I'd end up in the lake."

"Swimming?" Mitzi questioned.

Marla slapped her shoulder. "Good God, no. Bottom of the lake is what she means—with cement block shoes, I imagine. Oh shit, Molly. We must get you out of this mess."

"You need some serious money."

"Or we need to catch these guys at—something."

Molly thought for a minute. "I still have my job. And I suppose I could sell my Cadillac if I had to...."

One of Mitzi's brows raised. "Seriously? Can you raise that much cash selling Marty Lyn cosmetics? Plus, you need the caddy for work, so don't sell it. But being a consultant will not sustain your lifestyle, will it? I mean, I know you do well peddling mascara, but will it keep you in wine and manipedis and private school for the kids?"

"And pay off your tattooed debt collector?"

"Or Tom Purdy?"

"And keep Jackson Cooper at bay?"

Molly shook her head. "Unfortunately, no. The hard truth is the bank started foreclosure on the house last week. My checking account is nearly dry, and the credit cards were all cut off."

"You're broke."

"I'm broke." She took another gulp of her drink. "And worse, I had to ask Mom if I could move into Gran's house."

"Oh, God, you didn't. What did she say?"

"The usual. You know."

"We know," Marla and Mitzi echoed.

Molly closed her eyes and tipped back her head. As if the mess Don left her in wasn't bad enough, dealing with her mother's southern snark about nearly *everything-in-the-world* was a bit more than she could handle now. "I'm so screwed."

"Yep. Screwed like a pooch."

SERIOUSLY DEAD, BOOK 2

Get your copy at your favorite bookstore!

Do you get Maddie's VIP Insider News?

Be the first to get the latest news about my books—new releases, free ebooks, sales and discounts, sneak peeks, and exclusive content! Just add your email address at this link: https://maddiejamesbooks.com/pages/newsletter

Whether writing flirty contemporary romance or gritty romantic suspense, Maddie James writes to silence the people in her head.

In 2022, Maddie celebrated her 25th year of publishing romance fiction under multiple pen names. Her collective body of work includes over 70 titles. Maddie loves writing small town contemporary romance and cowboy worlds, and as M.L. Jameson she pens romantic suspense.

Affair de Coeur says Maddie, "shows a special talent for traditional romance," and RT Book Reviews claimed, "James deftly combines romance and suspense, so hop on for an exhilarating ride."

Do you get Maddie's VIP Insider News?

Learn more and buy books direct at www. maddiejamesbooks.com.